MANGO

By Pim Epler

Dedication

This book is dedicated to **Emily Whitney Epler**, our wild and high-spirited, energetic and curious, loving and caring daughter who was murdered on May 27, 2013. We never found out what happened. There were no witnesses. We cherish the 22 wonderful, exciting years we shared together. Our hearts are broken and always will be. As Reverend Crews said of her at her memorial service, "Emily was like a shooting star, rocketing through the night sky, lighting up the lives of everyone she met."

June 20, 1991 - May 27, 2013. RIP Emily. We love you.

This is a work of fiction. Names, characters, places and incidents are products of the author's imagination or are used fictitiously and are not to be construed as real. Any resemblance to actual events, locales, organizations, or persons, living or dead, is entirely coincidental.

ISBN:

ISBN-13: 978-0-9986939-1-0

The Bird

She moved like she don't care. Reckless. Quick, short steps. Straight into the South Florida jungle. Toward a teenage girl who was poking something on the ground.

"What the freak?" Cigarette ashes dropped into the unblinking eyes staring up at the young woman. Her cigarette wobbled in her lips, dropping more ashes into the eyes and onto the face.

"He's really cool looking," she said. "It's too bad he died." The ashes were landing on the corpse of a bird lying at her feet. It was a bird that did not belong in South Florida.

"Have you ever seen a bird like this before?" she said to the girl.

"Nope," Lisa said. "I've seen lots of birds, but none like this. It's not on the bird poster at the nature center."

"Crap, crap, crap." Emily threw her cigarette on the ground. She walked in a small circle, glancing back and forth into the woods.

Emily put another cigarette in her mouth and lit it. "This could really screw me up. It could ruin me. Bankrupt my parents. Shit."

Slashes of sun light meandered through the thick palm tree and live oak cover overhead and danced over the corpse. The sun was low to the east. The smell of new growth from palm trees and ferns stuck in the air. The vegetation held a vivid green from the March rains a day earlier.

Emily and Lisa were on a wooded plot of land on the western edge of Delray Beach, Florida. The land bordered a road that was flat and long, running straight for about half a mile before it curved back toward the east, toward the Atlantic Ocean, about ten miles away. The land on both sides of the road was covered with scrub brush, ferns, palm trees and live oak, and nothing else. No houses. No buildings. A residential neighborhood of medium sized one-story houses lay just on the other side of the curve in the road. A small mango farm operated a mile down the road in the other direction. Emily owned ten acres, about the size of a Walmart store and its parking lot.

Emily Whitney was 24 years old and had graduated 3 years earlier from Lynn University in Boca Raton with a B.S. degree in Business Administration. Her straight blond hair hung about 6 inches below her shoulders. She was 5 feet 6 inches tall, wiry, and had a gorgeous, slightly tanned face with a perfect complexion. She was in constant motion.

Emily glanced at the small pile of beer cans, pizza boxes and plastic bags lying near the road about 20 feet away. "Did you see who dumped that stuff?"

"No, but probably the redneck guys who hang out here at night in their pickups."

"How often do they come here?"

"Once a week or so, on Thursdays or Fridays. They don't do much. Just eat and drink, and play some shitty 70's music, and then they leave after about 45 minutes."

"Uh huh … well the town fines me for any garbage on the sides of the road."

She walked over to the garbage and scraped it into a large plastic trash bag, and then went back to the dead bird, took out her cell phone and took several pictures of it next to Lisa's foot to show the size of the bird. Then she brushed off the swarming flies, and pushed the carcass into the trash bag. Her throat and her gut twisted from the stench. Emily spit out an acidic gob onto the grass.

"Ha, ha, taste good?" Lisa said.

"Yummy. Want some? Hold out your hand. There's more where that came from."

"No way. Yuck. … My dad read about you trying to sell this lot, and he says he hopes the sale falls through."

"Why?"

"He said he likes open land, and he's afraid the traffic will go up from the new owners. I don't know… He can be a jerk sometimes and he never walks over here anyway. He usually just sits at home and watches football."

"He won't even notice any new traffic. The company buying the lot will only put in a small building. Most of the workers won't drive through your neighborhood. They'll come right off the highway. Tell him not to worry."

"Yeah - sometimes he just says or does things without thinking first. I'm surprised he hasn't been fired."

"What does he do?"

"He's a biology professor at Palm Beach State College."

"Sounds like an easy job. Well, thanks for calling me."

"Yeah … anytime. The town sucks. A-holes."

"Yeah, tell me about it."

"Freak, Freak, Freak!" Emily walked quickly toward her car. She heaved the trash bag in the trunk, got in the driver's seat, and slammed down the accelerator. She sped down the 25 mile-per-hour road doing 50. Driving fast relaxed her. She was oblivious to the people it might annoy, especially the local cops, whom she particularly disliked.

* * *

The 63 year old man ran through the sand and mud along the dry banks of Lake Mead at the tip of southern Nevada. Knee high scrub brush grew sparingly in the flat, sandy plain that abutted the lake. The sun was about six inches above the western horizon. An all-terrain vehicle 50 feet behind was chasing him. Whirling blades from wind turbines swooshed overhead.

He was panting heavily, and not moving fast. He was wearing camouflage pants, a camouflage shirt, a wide brimmed camouflage hat, and hiking boots. A camera with a large telescopic lens banged against his chest. Sweat dripped down his face and through his shirt. His face was grimacing. He would occasionally look back at the ATV.

The ATV had almost hit him 200 yards further up the trail, but the man had slid down the side of a 6 foot high rock to escape. Now they were on a flat, muddy trail.

The driver of the ATV glanced at the man every few seconds, but concentrated more on the *Maxim* magazine bouncing on his lap. The driver was wondering if the nearly naked bodies of the young ladies in the photos were natural or had been photo-shopped. He was sure they were natural. Teddy, the driver, kept the ATV at about one-quarter speed.

The man running on the flats was a member of the Nevada Raptor Federation, and the Federation was angry. The blades on the ten wind turbines operating nearby were decimating the local hawk, eagle, falcon and osprey populations. Man-made lakes had provided habits for the ospreys, and now man-made turbines were killing them en masse. A hawk would spot a rabbit, dive for it, and the unseen, giant whirling blades on the turbine would rip a wing off, and then the coyotes would finish the kill. The rabbit and rat populations near the turbines were booming, as was the number of rattlesnakes. Campers had learned to avoid the area.

The wind farm was owned by The Wind Reaper Incorporated. The company's logo was a silhouette of a fossil fuel worker whose head had just been lopped off by a wind turbine blade. The head, with a hard hat on top, was flying through the air a few feet off the torso. Underneath the slogan: "Renewable Energy, Savior of All People-Kind." There was a plaque near the farm entrance that read: "With special thanks to US Senator Hermey Reimthem for his work obtaining special tax credits and also Department of Energy subsidies, without which this wind farm would not be economically feasible."

Next to that was another plaque that read, "Financing provided by Stickler Hedge Fund, the Good Guys of Wall Street."

It was illegal for the wind farm company to accidentally kill these birds. They were protected by federal law. However, the Federal Government, in order to fight global warming, had given a waiver to the company, and so the company was slaughtering the birds. Not on purpose of course. Safeguards to protect the birds would be costly, and would reduce the moneys available for bonuses to the executives at the wind farm company.

Ermon Oil Company was not so lucky. Ten miles away, a dead crow was found in a small circle of oil, about a foot in diameter. A federal environmental protection agent found the corpse, and issued a $60,000 fine against the company. It was illegal for a fossil fuel company to kill any bird, and it did not matter whether the bird was endangered or not. Oil is evil, according to the pencil— pushers in Washington. Ermon Oil had appealed the fine, and argued that the federal department of agriculture had just poisoned 20,000 of the same type of crow in Kansas in order to protect cattle feed. Ermon lost the appeal, and paid the $60,000. The Democratic administration in Washington, D.C. detested oil companies, and also low oil prices. Low prices enabled the middle-class to waste money on heating and cooling their homes, driving to work and taking family vacations. Low oil prices also made wind and solar energy facilities ridiculously silly things to build ... except if you had government subsidies.

The Nevada Raptor Federation was staking out the wind farm, and filming the deaths and mutilations of the birds. The tearing apart by the coyotes made particularly riveting footage. The birders wanted to force the wind companies to add safety devices to protect the birds.

Adding safety devices was not financially feasible, and environmental groups and the government knew this. Environmental groups loved wind farms because the farms did not burn fossil fuels. The environmentalists did not like the Raptor Association filming the birds dying. The birders had to go. The environmentalists covered their faces with black bandannas and painted swastikas on their ATV's. White supremacist groups would be blamed.

Teddy's face was covered, and he was slowly chasing the birder gentleman. Teddy was 28 years old and worked at an environmentalist organization called The Enviro Hounds. As part of his job, he had come to Nevada to help the other environmentalists rid the area of the birders. Envir Hounds had received major charitable donations from the wind farm company. The wind farm company had received millions of dollars of federal government green-energy subsidies. The Democratic Party had received large contributions from both Enviro Hounds and the wind farm company.

The birder tripped on a log. Teddy was studying pictures of a young, scantily clad woman who was playing croquet against several other similarly dressed ladies. The birder lifted his face out of the mud, took off his muddy glasses, and yelled in terror when he saw through his blurred vision that the ATV was about to run him over.

Teddy looked up, saw the birder, and violently turned the steering wheel. The ATV smashed through a thicket of three foot high marsh grass and cattails. A small flock of birds went flying into the air. The ATV jolted to a halt in the mud. The wheels spun, but the ATV did not move. Teddy turned the engine off and stepped off. He chuckled as he pulled up the bandanna. That had been more fun than his normal work day at the office. The birder had gotten up out of the mud. He looked at Teddy, noticed the swastika on the ATV, turned and ran off.

Five minutes later a woman stopped her ATV 10 feet from Teddy's, and was laughing.

"How'd you do that Teddy?"

Teddy was smiling. "Throw me a rope and pull me out."

"I can't. You left them all tied to the bedposts in the hotel last night." She giggled.

"Ha, ha. I'm sure you have more in your trunk. You screamed like a night owl."

"You're an animal."

She took a rope out of the trunk of the ATV, secured one end to her tow bar, and threw it.

When Teddy went to pick up the rope he stepped on a dead bird. A few feet away he saw three other dead birds and two nests with broken eggs. The birds looked like common egrets from Florida.

He picked one up by its legs. "Well, it least we'll get dinner out of this."

"Freddy, that's a Yuma clapper rail. Shit Teddy."

"Yeah, so what? It's an egret, there are millions of them."

"Well, there are only about 800 Yuma clapper rails in existence, and you just killed one. They're on the endangered species list."

"No. I killed four."

"Holy cow, Teddy. The Feds just put an Indian medicine man in jail for 6 months just because he had one bald eagle feather in his headdress. He didn't even kill the eagle. Or so he said, and they didn't even accuse him of that."

"You mean a Native American?"

"Oh yeah, sorry Teddy. I didn't know you were so sensitive."

"Well, I didn't kill any birds. These bodies are going to disappear."

"What are you going to do? Eat them?"

The birder was a few hundred yards away taking pictures with his zoom lens.

After they freed the ATV, Teddy took the bodies back to his hotel room, put them on dry-ice in a thick plastic bag, and sent them back to his house in Florida in a well insulated Fed Ex box. The gators and snakes in the Florida swamps would enjoy the Nevada meat.

Teddy felt great. He had not had a rush of adrenaline like that since his college days. Breaking the law by threatening the old man. Breaking the law by killing and transporting an endangered species. Finally, getting away with both.

The Fed Ex box arrived at Teddy's house a week before Emily found the dead bird on her land.

* * *

Emily had a contract to sell her land to Wind Blades, Inc., a manufacturer of blades for wind turbines used to generate electricity. The company was moving from the high tax states of the northeast. They also needed to expand their capacity. Emily's lot was near interstate 95 and the Florida Turnpike, and not too far from some of their customers. A few days earlier Emily had received a letter from the City of Delray Beach stating that the city would have no objection to a reasonable increase in light truck traffic on the roads between the lot and the highways. The pieces for the sale of the land were falling into place.

After removing the garbage and the dead bird from the lot, Emily stopped at a Starbucks for a coffee in Boca Raton. She was sitting in her new black Honda Civic in the parking lot. She called Carla, her contact at Wind Blades Inc.

"Have you had a chance to look at the city clearance for the truck traffic?" Emily said.

"Yes. It looks great. Just what we needed."

"When can we close?"

"We're working on it. Hopefully we'll decide in a few weeks with a final closing in a month or two. You should know, Emily, that we are seriously looking at buying a different lot than the one you're selling in south Florida. A broker just brought it to our attention."

Emily straightened up in her car seat. She stared across the parking lot. "Oh." She took a sip of her coffee. "My lot is perfect for you. Where is the other lot?"

"In Boynton Beach. Not too far from your lot."

Emily threw her lighter against the passenger door. She breathed deeply, and stared out into the parking lot. "Well. Someone else is interested in buying my lot. They contacted my broker yesterday. I'll tell her to call the other buyer and see if they want to put in an offer."

"Sure. I understand. You need to do what you need to do. I'll let you know when we decide. Anything else, Emily?"

"No. Talk to you soon."

Emily's heart was pounding. If the sale fell through she would be ruined.

Her parents might lose $50,000. She might be stuck in an office job for life. She threw her coffee cup out the window.

*   *   *

Teddy arrived in his office overlooking The Intercoastal Waterway in Boca Raton at 9:05 in the morning. He closed and locked the door, stuck his face between the wooden breasts on the old mermaid bowsprit hanging on the wall, flicked the little dancing hula girl on his desk to get her swaying, turned on his laptop at a fairly high volume to last night's MSNBC, turned on the 50 inch high definition TV to the beautiful women on Fox News, with the sound off, turned on his high performance desktop computer, and plugged his headphones into his computer.

His fingers frantically pounded the keyboard. He stared intently at the screen. He smiled. "Got you, you dick-head."

His opponents in the Halo video game were college kids and some of his unemployed friends. He considered the game to be part of his workday. Video games sharpened his mind and quickened his decision making skills. He had read this in a defunct gaming magazine. MSNBC drowned out his chatter to the other gamers.

At 9:30 he shut off the electronics except for the muted FOX News, unlocked the door and started to read his work emails.

"Here's your coffee," said his 22 year-old assistant Lucita Rivera as she sashayed into Teddy's office. All thoughts immediately left Teddy's head, replaced by a kind of blank, warm nothingness, as he tried to only glance at her. His mouth could not formulate a "thank you," only a grunt indicating his thankfulness.

Her head turned to the reflection on the large exterior window when she walked toward the door. Teddy stared at the rhythm of her rear-end in the tight skirt. She always wore Latin styled business suits and low black leather stilettos.

Teddy's mind slowly left its state of pleasure and returned to equilibrium, as it had all of his life after a beautiful woman left his presence. He was used to it. *She knows she's tormenting me, and she's enjoying it.*

He turned his mind toward his future. He was the director of the local chapter of Enviro Hounds, a national environmentalist organization.

Teddy loved the agency, and it had been good to him. But he was bored. He was stationed in the small, Boca Raton office, and needed to move up in the organization. His goal was to get promoted to a regional office, and then to the central headquarters in Washington, D.C. A swarm of environmentalists had graduated from America's colleges in the years before Teddy graduated, making it difficult for Teddy to move up. He had to distinguish himself.

Many of these graduates had wanted to get jobs in the big oil companies. Their college political science and sociology professors had encouraged their students to destroy the oil companies from within, as employees. The students liked the jobs because they paid well. Unfortunately, almost all of the students were unable to pass the basic science and math classes needed to work for an oil company. So they migrated to jobs at environmentalist non-profits where the hiring standards required neither science nor math.

The pending sale of Emily's lot had received strong local publicity because of the good jobs the buyer would bring into Delray Beach. If Teddy could get some national publicity by blocking the sale, the higher-ups would notice him, admire his tenacity, and doors would open in the regional or national offices.

He had planted the dead bird at the beginning of a hiking trail in a small clearing. He had told one of his staff, Sam, to go to the trail because he had heard a rumor that there were rare ground-nesting birds on the lot.

* * *

Sam walked into Teddy's office. "I was just at that lot you asked me to go to, and didn't see any rare birds. Man, did you see Lucita this morning? I'm going to have to learn Spanish."

"Que grande, eh senior?"

"Si. Si."

"No birds? A friend of mine said he saw some odd birds there a few days ago."

"No. No birds at all. Rare or un-rare."

"Did you look on the ground? He said they nested on the ground. He saw them at the beginning of that trail that goes into the lot."

"No. They're not there anymore. But it was great to get out of the office early, so if you need me to go out in the field again, I'd love to."

"Thanks. Maybe you'd like to do some field work with Lucita. The birds might be hiding in the bushes."

"I think I should find out."

"I'll go by the lot this afternoon and see if I can see any."

The Pick Up

On Thursday nights Teddy enjoyed going out to the bars in Delray Beach and Boca Raton. His main goals in life were to build a large bank account, to score with women, and to become a powerful environmentalist so that he could make even more money. He admired Al Gore for turning green into green.

The local young female lawyers liked to let off steam toward the end of a stressful week. Teddy found them easy pickings. He was not sure why this was so, but he had his theories. The lady lawyers had many career frustrations. Most had student loans totaling between $150,000 to $200,000 that would take 20 years to pay off. Their jobs usually paid between $45,000 and $70,000. This was much lower than what they had expected when they had applied to law school. Their hours were long, the work was boring, and many of the clients were obnoxious. The clients did not believe they should have to pay fees much above what they paid a lawn-care man. Some clients even thought the lawyers should work for free because the lawyers had an obligation to give back to society. The clients often earned more than the lawyers, drove better cars and lived in nicer houses.

Since the 2008 recession the plight of lawyers had gotten even worse. There had been massive lay offs and high unemployment. Wages and the ability to charge clients had fallen.

For Teddy, it was like shooting fish in a barrel. The young ladies were frustrated with their careers, and wanted to reduce their stress. Teddy loved the pretty ones, but he often had to settle for the slightly plump, mediocre ones. When he was particularly horny, he would go home with almost anything that moved and had half a brain.

He parked his car in downtown Boca Raton and walked by the Ram Rod and Les Bos bars. He had never been in either, and was tempted to go in, but he got a strange feeling when he looked in the windows. At Les Bos the men were mostly short, had no facial hair, and dressed in baggy clothes that were not particularly stylish. There were no tall, muscular men like you see in most

Florida bars. It seemed like most of the clientele were women. Those who saw him turned away.

The guys at the Ram Rod however got very excited when they saw Teddy gaze in the window, and several gave him a welcoming wave. One even blew Teddy a kiss. Teddy saw no women.

He chose the Wicked Mermaid. In the entrance was a small fountain with a 3 foot high mermaid statue with a mischievous grin on her face, and water gently shooting out of her nipples in a low arc into a pool. He immediately felt relaxed as he took in the dim lights of the room shining from a high ceiling, the chatter of the people, the clicking of glasses, and the movements of the bartenders. The shiny, copper bar was the length of two BMW sedans. On the walls were art deco prints of buildings from New York City and Miami. The crowd was mostly under the age of 40. The cocktails were specialty ones, and cost $5 more than the drinks at an average bar.

He picked an open spot at the bar near three attractive women who were about 23 years old.

"A Slippery Nipple please," he said to the bartender.

"Heard of them but don't know how to make them," she said. "Sorry. Too busy to look it up tonight."

"OK. A Sex on the Beach please."

"Are you kidding me? No one ever orders either of those drinks. You seem to have something on your mind."

She gazed at his face and then at his body. "Do you want to meet me after work ... on the beach?" She was about 45 years old, and pretty. She would be a reserve player for the end of the evening if nothing better came along. *Nothing like a good MLF. They know how to get things done.*

"I apologize," Teddy said. "I had no hidden meanings. They are fun to order, though. OK. Do you have any specialty cocktails?"

"Yes, an Abby Road, a Mexicana, a Delray Mule and a few others. They're listed on the right front side of the wine list."

"Uh ... I'll have an Abby Road, please."

"OK. Later I'll look up how to make a Sex On The Beach, if you're still interested." She smiled at him.

"Sounds good. A little sand in strange places is good for the soul. I'll have to see if I'm still thirsty at that hour."

"You look like you're always thirsty." She smiled, turned and grabbed a bottle of gin from the neat line of spirits behind the bar.

The fresh lemon juice, muddled mint leaves, apple juice, candied ginger and gin of the Abby Road hit Teddy's taste buds. He slowly sipped it. He relaxed. He enjoyed the atmosphere of the bar.

His phone vibrated. The text message said, "Stop stalking me you crepo or I'll get a restraining order." *She still loves me. I know*. The sender had dumped

Teddy two years ago. He had been very attached to her, and still thought about her often.

He was not very good with opening lines, but he always came up with something. Usually something lame. His good looks, 6 foot 1 inch frame, slender muscular build, and stylish attire were usually good enough for him to get past his weak opening line.

"Do you go to Florida Atlantic?" he said to closest of the three young women standing next to him at the bar.

She turned slightly toward him, looked at his face, and then ran her eyes down his body, and said, "No." She then turned so that her back was facing Teddy, and said to her friends, "So do you want to go to the Lynn men's soccer game tomorrow?"

Teddy was not discouraged. He knew she was out of his league - too young, good looking and cheerful. Also he was usually more successful if he had a wing-man. Girls were less suspicious of guys who were with friends. The guys were less likely to be weirdos. Plus he liked to chat with someone while he was hunting.

At about 10:00 the bar began to thin out. Most people had work or college classes the next day. Like dusk for the sharks swimming in the Atlantic a mile away, this was the time of the night that Teddy was most successful. He had a slight buzz from the four cocktails he had drunk in an hour and a half. They had varied from gin to tequila to rum to Southern Comfort. He drank the Southern Comfort because he loved their ad with the slightly over-weight, middle-aged man in a long style Speedo walking down the beach with cool music playing in the background, holding a cocktail class with Southern Comfort on ice. He always chuckled when he saw that ad, no matter how often he saw it.

At 10:30 he saw his mark. Three women in their mid- 20's moved from a table to the bar, and they seemed to be drunk. Not horribly drunk, but definitely drunk. They were dressed like lawyers - somewhat neat, but not stylish, and a little dowdy. Off-the-rack from Macy's. Why waste money on good clothes when you represented drunk drivers, home owners who could not pay their mortgages, and car accident drivers? They were a little over-weight, not unattractive, and oozing with sexuality, at least in Teddy's eyes. At their ages their urge to find a husband and have children was boiling over. Teddy would be that man … for tonight.

Teddy was watching the college basketball game on the TV near him. The Miami Heat was on the TV near the girls. He moved to an empty spot near the girls but stared at the game and did not look at the girls. He said, "yes!" when a Heat player scored, and cursed about the officiating when a call went against the Heat. The girls' circle slowly opened up.

One of the ladies glanced at him. A few minutes later she said to Teddy, "So do you think they'll win? The Thunder are pretty good."

"Yea, they'll pull it off. With Wade and Bosch they're pretty tough."

They watched the next play, and then the girl said, "He should have taken the 2 instead of the 3 point shot."

"Yea, but they say it's better to take 3's than 2's. You miss more, but it's better over-all."

"Yea. Definitely."

And so the evening went, and Teddy was soon flirting with the entire gang.

Three of the four girls flirted with Teddy. The fourth spent a lot of time on her cell phone. She said to the group, "Sam is flying in tomorrow at 10:00 to Ft. Lauderdale."

One of the girls, Brittany, was standing closer to Teddy than the others and would bump into him once in awhile and squeeze his arm. She laughed at all his jokes, taunted him and gave him her full attention and smile. "Teddy, that's stupid." Then a beaming smile. Like most men receiving such attention, Teddy became aroused, and lost his ability to think straight. The predator became the prey. He knew he was now the prey, and he liked being the prey. He felt tingling sensations. Being the prey also meant almost guaranteed success. But not all the time.

Teddy preferred one of the others a little more than Brittany, but he thought Brittany would do just fine. Around 11:30 everyone said they needed to go home for work the next day.

Brittany said to the girls, "I'll see you tomorrow. I'm just going to finish my wine. Good night." They left.

"I'm leaving after this drink too." Teddy took a sip of his Coca-Cola, no alcohol. "Are you a lawyer?"

Brittany was about four years younger than the others, pretty. In fairly good shape. Slightly plump.

"No. Why did you think I was a lawyer?"

"I don't know. I've met lawyers here before."

"Have you? Really? You like women lawyers? You like women bossing you around?"

"Sometimes it can be fun. Usually I enjoy being in charge."

Brittany smiled. "I sense a little conflict coming on."

Teddy smiled. "We might have to settle this with a little wrestling match."

"I'd go for that. My scissor-hold is painful."

"Ooo. Ouch."

They both took sips from their drinks.

"So … no. I'm not a lawyer. I've only been out of college a few years, and work for a small company that my friend started in college."

"What does the company do?"

"The company has two totally different businesses. We sell specialty marine products, and we also provide cleaning services for the weekly condo rental market. I like it, but it's not very stable."

"Well, it sounds better than being a lawyer like your friends."

"Yeah - no kidding. Don't know what they were thinking. And they all have huge student debt that they can't pay. It's not all their fault - they believed what the so-called experts and our great President said, that 'you need to get a good education in order to make it in this modern economy.' I have lots of friends who never went to college who earn more than my lawyer friends. It's sad. But what can you do? Not my problem."

"Yeah, that blows." Teddy finished his Coca-Cola. "Well, I'm out of here. Can I walk you to your car?"

"Yes. Thanks. That would be nice."

When they got to the car Teddy asked, "There are some good March Madness games on. Do you want to come to my house to watch a few?"

"It's late, but maybe we can see the end of a few games. Florida State I think is playing at Stanford. So they started late. Sure."

* * *

Teddy had rented a small three bedroom ranch house in a quiet, nondescript neighborhood in Boca Raton. He and Brittany went into the house and then to the kitchen. He kept it clean. It was small but had been modernized with a stainless steel stove, refrigerator and oven. The counter-tops were a green speckled marble, and the cabinets were cherry.

"I'm going to make popcorn. Do you want anything to drink?" Teddy said.

"Water please."

She looked at the photos stuck to his refrigerator. Then she saw a copy of a college diploma on the fridge listing Teddy's name.

"That's cool. You keep a copy of your diploma on the fridge? Brown University? I hear that's a pretty good school. Somewhere in California, right? The Golden State Brown Bears?"

"No. That's the University of California Golden Bears. Brown is in Rhode Island."

She's not a ditz, but the people down here, not knowing Brown University? But when it snows three feet in the northeast, this is the place to be.

Teddy poured the waters, he and Brittany went into his living room. There was a deep cushioned black couch, a 60 inch high definition TV, and the room was clean and neat. Teddy turned on the basketball game.

She had not seemed impressed by his Brown University diploma. His Brown diploma was a key to unlocking a young woman's legs. No key tonight. Brown University implied high income potential. Money to some women was like pollen to a bee. Add some smooth talking, and an impressive environmentalist job, and Kazam, that's all it would usually take.

The Brown University move had worked well in New England with the girls from the local colleges, like Wheaton, Boston College and Brandeis. It didn't work well with the girls from Florida. Few Florida girls had heard of Brown, let alone of the Ivy League. They were not impressed. Besides, many of their moms and dads had done quite well graduating from Florida Atlantic, The University of Florida, Flagler College and Lynn University. Why go to Brown?

Luckily for Teddy, Brittany was horny and she did not seem to care what college he had graduated from, or the fact that he worked at an environmental agency. He was a catch. He had a job, half a brain, dressed OK, showered, was not obese or emaciated, was not a Florida odd-ball, was less than 35 years old, and could form thoughts and even express them.

As they watched the game, she grabbed his knee every time Florida State scored. He immediately became aroused, and his brain became fuzzy. He was, however, able to follow the game. With 3 seconds to go, Florida State was down by 2. Florida took a 3 point shot and it swished through the net. The stadium went wild. So did Brittany. She pushed Teddy onto his back before the announcer could say, "Wow! What a game!" Teddy had tried to stammer, "Wow! What a game!" but Brittany's lips were locked onto his before he could get the words out.

Ah Oh ... We're Going Down

Emily worked at a small marketing company in Boynton Beach where she was the head of social media marketing. She promoted her clients through Facebook, Twitter, Tumbler and similar websites. Her clients were local small businesses like dentists, doctors and lawyers, restaurants, gentlemen's clubs, hair stylists, bait shops and marinas.

The two seascape prints hanging on her white office walls had been there when Emily had started the job. A laptop computer and a family picture of herself, and her younger brother, mother and father were the only things on the desk other than a light. A window overlooked the courtyard of a condo complex.

She arrived at work at 8:30, called a few clients, and returned some emails. Then she called the banker who had helped her get the loan to buy the lot. The lot was her personal business.

Gabrielle said, "What can I do for you?"

"The sale of the lot is still going forward but it seems to be taking longer than I thought it would. The first monthly mortgage payment comes due in about 3 weeks, and I'm sure I'll be able to make it, but just to be safe, would the bank be willing to extend the first payment date out about a month?"

"No way," Gabrielle said. "You know that we stuck our necks out to approve this loan to you, and we were always very clear that payments needed to be made on time."

"Yes, but well ... I don't see how the bank will be hurt if I pay a few months late. Of course I'll pay the extra interest that comes due. It would really help me."

"No, sorry. Your mortgage is one of our first under this new bank mortgage program. The program is for young, local business people. The loan needs to stay squeaky clean so that the higher ups don't get worried and end the whole program."

"Can you ask your boss?"

"No, not now. Do what you can to save money for that first payment. If things don't get better for you in a month or so I might be able to talk to my boss. But he was never a big fan of this loan program, and actually didn't like the loan for your project all that much. So don't count on him bailing you out."

Bitch. "Thanks. Bye."

Crap. No payments were due on the loan for 4 months. Then monthly payments became due, and in 10 months the entire loan would come due. However, Emily's cash flow was not good. The payments would have to come from her savings and from whatever was left from her paychecks from her marketing job. Her parents had signed a partial guarantee of the loan for $50,000 out of the entire amount. The loan would not have been approved without the guarantee. She loved her parents, and knew that if she defaulted on the loan, and they had to pay the $50,000, they'd really feel the pain. They were close to retirement, and would have to work a few more years to make up for the loss. Plus, what would they think of her? That she was a disappointment? A failure?

She was terrified of working for someone else, sitting in a cubicle, in some building from 8:30 to 5:30 each day, taking orders from some buffoon of a boss. *For thirty years. Yuk, yuk, yuk.* She was only 24 years old, and the mere thought of the cubicle made her nauseous. Dismayed. Disenchanted. Disillusioned. That is not what her high school and college professors had said life would be like. How had her mom and dad done it for so long? Work in an office, year after year, with only small advancements every few years to slightly higher positions that were only marginally more interesting and challenging?

Her parents were either stronger than her, or had slowly gone a little crazy dealing with the monotony. She was pretty sure they had gone a little crazy. Especially her father who would crack one-line jokes that he would laugh at while those around him would pretend they did not hear it, or would mumble under their breathes, "that's disgusting." *Well, at least he enjoys himself.* She found the jokes to be pretty funny, which made her wonder a little about herself.

And to make it even worse, she and her parents had watched less talented people get better and more interesting positions because of their connections. Sure, Chelsea Clinton and the Bush daughters were smart and pleasant, but would they have gotten their great jobs without their parents' connections? There were plenty of other Yale graduates that were at least as talented as they were. And how about the Hollywood elite getting their grown children acting jobs? Ahead of all those other starving, talented young actors. She had not liked the "Occupy Wall Street" movement, but they did have a point regarding elitist nepotism.

Selling the lot at a decent profit was her first step in avoiding the boredom of a cubicle life. It would be a step toward running her own business and her own life, and toward making a decent living.

* * *

The dead bird bothered Emily all day long. She didn't know why. It looked like an egret but there was something a little different about it. Lisa had thought it did not look right.

Serious bird watching was not one of her hobbies, but she enjoyed watching them fly and eat the crabs and small fish in the marshes. The lightning fast legs of the sandpipers running along the edge of the surf were always entertaining. Why a particular bird would choose to run to the right and not to the left mystified her. The choice had nothing to do with instinct, like a bird knowing how to build a nest. Or like a spider's instinctive ability to weave a web. The bird had quickly made a choice to turn right, not left. What had gone through its mind to make that choice? Who knew?

She loved animals and volunteered with a local conservation group to help protect nesting sea turtles on the Boca Raton beaches. She also volunteered at the Gumbo Limbo Nature Center, educating visitors about the animals in the petting tanks. She donated $10 a year to the center.

She had followed global warming in the news, and was a little worried about its effects on Florida because Florida was so close to sea level. She had not noticed any changes at the beaches or along the bulkheads on the Intercoastal Waterway. But she had read that the increase in the sea level would be so slow that you would not notice it. So how did the scientists accurately measure the sea level when the size of the tides was always changing with the moon, and with the winds and the weather? Also the sands on the beaches were constantly shifting. The scientists must know what they are doing. What do they do if they disagree on a sea level measurement? How do they resolve the disagreement and come up with a measurement number? Why did they predict in the 1970's that there would be a new ice age, and we would all starve? Well, the rich environmentalists like Al Gore wouldn't starve. Not her problem.

Back to the bird. She could not stop thinking about the bird. She really needed the lot sale to go through. She needed to stop worrying about the bird.

She had taken a biology course in college, and had gotten along well with the professor, Professor Robinson. The professor also volunteered at the nature center, and Emily would see her every so often at the center and small-talked with her. So Emily emailed the professor, reminded her that she had taken her biology course at Lynn University, and that they worked together at the nature center. Emily attached a picture of the bird. She added that the carcass was in a plastic bag in her freezer. She asked the professor if she could identify the bird.

The professor emailed back saying that it looked much like a common

Florida egret, but there was something a little different about it. Could Emily drop off the carcass to the professor's office? Professor Robinson would have to do some research and talk to some bird watcher friends of hers. She would get back to Emily. Later that day Emily drove to the college and left the carcass with Professor Robinson's assistant.

* * *

The next day during lunch time Emily went to a meeting at a company called Mermaid Inc. Mermaid Inc. was managed by one of Emily's old college friends, Jerry, out of his home office.

Emily was impressed that there were only a few small stacks of papers piled on his desk, and that most of the invoices and orders had been filed in the wood veneer filing cabinet. Hanging on the wall was a painting of a mermaid in bright coral reef colors. Her eyes followed you as you moved. On the desk was a boat cleat with a small mermaid statue welded to the top.

It was not much of a company, and barely covered its expenses and payroll. But it did manage to limp along each month. Emily had started it in college to help pay for her tuition. The company subcontracted with a small forge in Ft. Lauderdale to manufacture decorative boat cleats. On the cleats was a smiling mermaid with long flowing red hair and a twisting mermaid tail. The mermaids all had white skin, large deep blue eyes, ruby red lips and an aqua-green tail. People bought them to tie up blinds and shades in their homes, and also to secure boats, usually small ones, to docks. The cleats added a little color and pizzazz to the marinas, and the little kids liked them.

Emily had made a small profit each month, and the money helped to pay her bills. More importantly, she had found that the business had looked good on her resume when she had tried to get a job at graduation. Potential employers could look at her website. She used it to market herself as being aggressive, proactive and skilled with Internet marketing techniques.

In order to try to increase profits, Emily and her partners had expanded the business to include cleaning services for condo owners between Deerfield Beach and Delray Beach. The owners rented their units out on a weekly basis. They needed someone to clean the units at the end of each weekly rental. This business proved more lucrative than the decorative cleat business, but it required more people than did the cleat business.

Mermaid Inc's third line of business was selling two items over the internet, a beach game and a back shaver for hairy-backed men. Jerry made both in his apartment. The game consisted of a net with poles, like a small badminton net, except it had smaller holes and was skinnier. They marketed the net as a game you can use with the standard wooden beach paddles and small rubber ball. They sold the game at www.beachpaddletennis.com and on Amazon. Sales were horrible.

The back shaver however racked up good sales. Some sales went to men, but most went to older women and also to pregnant women. Sales took off when AARP mentioned the back shaver in a small joke article in its news letter. They said it would be a smart Christmas stocking-stuffer, as they cost only $11.99, plus $2.85 for shipping and handling. The ladies found the article offensive, but they loved the razor extender because it was hard to reach the stubble at the bottom of their calves. There was plenty of man-action at the retirement communities, and the ladies needed to be at the top of their games. After all, you only live once. Mermaid Inc. sold the games at www.silkyback.com and also on Amazon.

Emily owned Mermaid Inc but did not manage it. She had started the company by herself while in college. It expanded and she hired people, and then she slowly became less involved. Her classmates from college, Jerry and Brittany ran it. Three other college friends worked there part time. They used subcontractors to clean most of the condominiums.

Emily and Brittany sat down on the couch in the office, waiting for Jerry to come in from the kitchen. They had been good friends for about six years, but had not seen each other for several weeks.

"So how are you doing?" Emily said.

"Not bad. And you?"

"Ok. Trying to sell that land I bought. It's really stressful."

"I can't believe you stuck your neck out and bought that. Can't believe any bank was stupid enough to give you a loan."

Emily laughed. "Me neither. I don't know what bankers are thinking. Mortgages are all new to me. I guess the bankers know what they're doing. Going for big bonuses by giving out silly loans probably…. So do you go out at all to the bars anymore?"

"Yeah. A few times a week. Mostly Thursdays and Saturdays. Usually with some people I know from FAU."

"Where do you go?"

"All over. Delray. Boca. But I stay away from the college bars, and try to go more upscale places where the local business people hang out."

"Have you met anybody you like?"

"Some of the guys we go out with are really nice. A little immature. But fun. I met this guy the other night. Teddy. I liked him. Pretty normal. I thought we had a great time. But he hasn't texted me back."

"Well you only met him at a bar. Maybe he's married."

"No. He's not married. We did a little more than just meet at a bar."

"Oh. Yeah. OK. He really should text you back. I've met a few pricks who don't. A-holes."

"He didn't seem like an A-hole. We'll see if he gets back to me in the next few days. Plus he runs a local environmentalist non-profit. You'd think a guy like that would be better than your average creep."

"You'd hope so. I'm sure he is. He's probably been busy at work, and will text you today."

"Yea."

Jerry walked in with three coffees.

"So are we making any money?" said Emily.

"Well, some money is coming in," Jerry said. "We're paying my salary and Brittany's. We're paying John, Maria and Sara, and the cleaning contractors. And we're paying for our cost of goods - basically the mermaid cleats. But the account is short a little every month. Probably because of miscellaneous costs like office supplies, gas for our cars and things like that."

"Damn, Jerry," Emily said. "I've been giving, I mean loaning, money to the company for about five months. It's really adding up, and draining me."

"Yeah. Brittany and I appreciate it ... a lot. I really need this job. The economy blows. The government is lying when they say the unemployment rate is getting better. Most college grads I know are living at home and have jobs that high school kids could do. Boring jobs as well."

"We really appreciate it Emily," Brittany said. "This job means a lot to me too. Not just the money, but it looks good on my resume. Being on unemployment would look really bad when I start looking for more of a corporate job."

"Yea, I know," said Emily. "How much does the company need this month?"

"$100," Jerry said.

"Man … that's $20 more than last month. We're heading in the wrong direction." Emily took a sip of coffee.

"Maybe if we make some small adjustments we can get in the black," Brittany said. "I know we're working on bare-bones."

"I really should be paid more for running this out of my apartment," Jerry said. "You know, rent."

Emily smiled at Jerry.

"We use eco-friendly cleaning fluids to clean the condos," Brittany said. "If we switch to standard cleaning fluids, we'd save about $75 a month. I've run the numbers on the amount of cleaners we use and the cost per bottle."

"No way," Emily said. "We're going to stick with the eco-friendly stuff. I don't want to pour some chemical crap down the drains."

"Yea, but you have another job and don't need the money from this business," Brittany said. "If you get tired of cutting checks to Mermaid each month, it folds, and we lose our jobs."

Emily said, "Don't worry. We'll talk first before it folds."

"Your environmentalist friends from that college group you were in twisted your thinking," Jerry said. "They were pretty hard core. They hated me. They got really pissed when I asked them some questions about CO2 and fracking. Didn't they recommend the enviro cleaning fluids to you? They probably were just repeating some babble someone else had told them. They didn't seem to have brains of their own. Are the eco-friendly cleaning fluids really eco-friendly, or is it just more BS marketing, like solar energy and electric cars?"

Emily said, "Hey. They were really nice people, and the eco-friendly stuff is really good stuff."

Jerry said, "I have a friend who's a big environmentalist. He's a really nice guy but once he asked me why I still use plastic bags from the grocery store. He bought re-usable bags. I pointed out to him that it might take more pollution to make his sturdy bags than to make my thin bags, that I also recycle. The guy went berserk, and started yelling at me at the top of his lungs. Seriously. The vein on his forehead was popping out and throbbing. His face was bright red, and he was slurring his words. I could barely understand a thing he said. It was not exactly a reasoned debate between two rational people. We don't talk about environmental issues anymore."

"So are they Jerry?" Brittany said.

"Are they what?"

"Are the throw-away recyclable bags from the grocery store better for the environment than the reusable one?" Brittany said.

"How the F do I know?" Jerry said. "I just wanted to see what he would say. Last time I'll do that. I still use the free throw-away bags, and I recycle them - most of the time."

"Thanks for that fascinating story," Emily said. We're staying with the enviro friendly cleaning fluids. But I know what you mean. When I was about 10 years old my parents started an environmental non-profit in Westchester County in southern New York. They were trying to block a developer from dredging a salt marsh so it could be used as a harbor for tankers. They did block the developer. But later some extremist environmentalists joined the group. They thought my parents were too easy-going, and they threw may parents out."

Why don't Jerry and Brittany volunteer to take $50 per month pay cuts? Then the company won't fold.

"OK," Emily said. "Let's get back to our money problems. How are the sales for the mermaid cleats?"

"They are OK, but are slowly going down every month," Jerry said.

"Do you have any idea why?" Emily said. "Any ideas on how to reverse the trend?"

"I'll call some of the stores and marina's to see if their customers have had any complaints," Brittany said. "We could also set up a blog on our website for customer feedback."

"Yeah - we need to do something," Emily said. "Selling the mermaid cleats is the main reason I keep pumping money into this. If it gets popular nationally, we could make a lot of money off Internet sales, unless those A-holes in Washington force us to pay local sales taxes. Then we'll have to fold. No one else is selling cleats like ours. Making money off condo cleaning is nice and steady, but we could never hit a home run like if we sold a million cleats."

"Yeah," Brittany said. "I love to dream. Especially about money."

"How are we doing with the condo cleaning, and also with the selling of the beach net games?" Emily said.

"Our customer base with the condos is steady, and we add a new condo owner once every few months," Jerry said. "We make money off each unit cleaned even after you factor in the cost of the subcontractors and the cleaning product costs.

"We're selling almost no beach net games, but we essentially have no monthly costs since we bought all the material to make the nets a year ago, and we have lots of extra material. The cost of the pipes is really cheap. One inch pvc pipes from HomeDepot. We buy them as needed - which is almost never."

"That's a disappointment," Emily said. "And how about the Silky Back back shaver sales?"

"Really solid, but our profit margins are thin on each sale," Jerry said. "We should play with upping the price."

"OK. That's good on the condo cleaning," Emily said. "I'm not worried about the beach net game. That's more of a hobby and there are no costs really. On the back shavers let's increase the price by $1.25, and see what happens to sales. What do you guys think?"

Brittany and Jerry both agreed.

"Well, if we ever start making money off the beach game and off the back shaver, remember that I put the time in to make them, and wasn't paid," Jerry said.

"We won't forget, Jerry," Brittany said.

"OK, if there's nothing else, I've got to run," Emily said.

On her way home Emily calculated how long she could keep on writing checks to keep Mermaid Inc alive. One hundred bucks a month was not a lot of money for many people, but for her it was. But then again, her cigarette expenses were even worse. Jerry and Brittany were good friends from college and Emily knew they needed the jobs. Plus, the job market for college graduates had been horrible since the 2008 housing crash. She wanted Mermaid LLC to be able to hire more Lynn University graduates as a kind of launching pad for them to get jobs at more stable companies. Mermaid LLC was a way for her to 'give back' as they say, rather than a money maker. Although, she thought, it might actually make money someday, especially with beachpaddletennis.com and SilkyBack.com.

* * *

* * *

After the meeting with Jerry and Brittany, Emily returned to her job at the marketing company. Her phone buzzed. It was Professor Robinson.

"Well. That bird is really odd. It's definitely not a Florida egret. Our egrets have a different shaped beak and different shaped feet. So I looked in some of my bird books and did some research. It is a Yuma clapper rail."

"A Yuma clapper rail? Never heard of that."

"That's not surprising, unless you live in Utah or Arizona or thereabouts. I sent the picture to a colleague in the bio department at the University of Nevada, and he confirmed it was a Yuma clapper rail."

"Well, I guess it decided to migrate to Florida for the winter, like all those snowbirds from New York."

"I don't think so. My U. Nevada contact said they rarely migrate, and if they did, it would be to Mexico, not Florida. Just look on a map. It would make no sense for a bird to fly from Nevada to Florida. Mexico is much easier."

"Maybe it was flying to Mexico and a storm blew it off course."

"I've never heard of a Yuma being seen around here. I called the Florida Audubon Society, and the University of Florida bio department, and neither had ever heard of a Yuma in Florida. They didn't even know what a Yuma is."

"Well, so not a problem. I won't find any more on my land."

"Yes and no. It has the potential to be a big problem, but it's unlikely."

"Oh crap. I don't need any more problems. Why?"

"Because they are almost extinct. There are only 800 or so as far as people know, and they all live in the states around Nevada."

"Oh shit! So they're on the endangered species list?"

"Afraid so."

"I might become an endangered species if I go bankrupt. If the Yuma has decided to re-locate to Florida, to my land, the feds and the state will block me from developing my land. No one will buy it. The bank will demand money from my parents. This could really suck. I think I'll go buy a shot gun to … uh … scare the Yumas away."

"Please don't do that. Be careful, because the fines for hurting an endangered species, just one, are huge. And more fines for harming their habitat."

"Florida is not their habitat. The desert is."

"Not the desert. Marshes in the desert, near ponds and lakes."

"Those are different from Florida marshes. Ours are salty or brackish."

"Did you ever hear of the Great Salt Lake? You know, where a lot of Mormons live. Actually, I don't know if the birds live there. Don't know enough about them or the lake for that matter … Hmm … Good idea for a field trip, paid for by a government grant."

"Can I come as your research assistant? Free of charge?"

"No. You were a business major, from what I can remember."

"So you don't think I have a serious problem. Maybe I shouldn't worry too much."

"Not for now, and I doubt ever. Probably no more Yumas will be found near here. I don't have an obligation to report it to the state unless you ... actually I, find more. I won't be out looking for them. They don't belong here. This was an aberration."

"Definitely. A freak of nature. Darwin run amok, or something like that."

"You won't find any more, I'm sure. I'd love to know how it got there. They aren't like the cuddly pythons that some of our eccentric Floridians neighbors have as pets. I don't know who would want a Yuma as a pet. A parrot, yes. A Yuma no. You'd have to feed them marsh worms."

Emily looked out her office window. "I like my pet python. Plan to let it go near Lynn University when it gets too big for me to handle. It wrapped around me last night, but I had a knife and was ready to cut off its head." She laughed.

"Can't wait to see it crawling around campus."

"I'm only joking. Its not a python, it's a boa, and it's only two feet long."

"Glad you still have your sense of humor. It livened up my class you took -- for everyone. But anyway, I still would love to know how that bird got on your land. Does anyone hate you? Do you have competition from someone else trying to sell their land to your buyer?"

"There are a few people who I'm sure hate me, but they are too stupid ... actually, not stupid, unsophisticated would be a better word ... to plant an endangered species on my land. They are more into slashing tires, and keying cars and that type of thing. Old girlfriends of guys I've dated. Jealous drunken rage behavior."

"Nice. I was young once. I guess we were just as ... well ... rowdy. Hard for me to picture now, with cell phones and Facebook. You can wreck havoc with the toys you guys have now."

Emily swung her chair back facing her desk. "Tell me about it. It's a jungle out there. Keep in touch. See you at Gumbo Limbo one of these days. Thanks a lot for all your work professor. See you around."

"Anytime. It was fun to do the research. A change of pace."

* * *

Emil stopped at the Publix Super Market on her way home from work to buy some groceries and saw her academic adviser from when she was in college, Professor Sanchez. She had taken four business courses with him.

"Professor Sanchez! How are you? Remember me?"

"Sure Emily. I wouldn't forget you. You were probably my noisiest student ever. I mean that in a good way."

"Ha. Ha. Thanks."

"I liked it. You always raised your hand a lot, and participated in class discussions. Professors like participation. How are you doing?"

"I'm doing well, thanks. I'm working at a small marketing company, and I have a few other things going on on the side to help pay the bills. I use a lot of what I learned from your courses in my job."

"That makes me feel good. I read in the newspaper that you're trying to sell your land to a wind blade manufacturer."

"Yea. That's me."

"Boy. You bit off a lot for someone as young as you when you bought that land. How's the sale going?"

"Pretty well. Some bumps here and there. I hope it sells in the next few months. It should. It's scary having that mortgage hanging over my head."

"I'm still amazed you were able to buy the lot. You don't have a long credit history."

"I was lucky. I couldn't have done it without the loan program that the bank set up with the college. Also, my parents are on the hook, but not for the entire amount."

"Well, if there's anything I can do to help, give me a call at my office. Or if you just want to strategize, just call. When you make your first million, don't forget Lynn University can always use a donation, especially the business department. Good luck with the sale."

"I won't forget. It was good seeing you."

* * *

A few days later The Palm Beach Post had a picture of the dead Yuma clapper rail with a small article about the unusual bird. It said, in part:

What will those wild snowbirds bring us next? Well it appears they have brought us an endangered cousin of theirs. A bird that inhabits only Nevada, Utah and Arizona was found on an empty lot on the western edge of in Delray Beach. The Audubon Society has verified that the bird was a Yuma clapper rail. A spokesperson for the Society said it is a critically endangered species and there are only about 800 still in existence, all in western states. How it got to Florida is a mystery. It is highly unlikely that it flew here on its own. Apparently it did not like our beautiful Florida weather, since it was dead when found.

The Delray bar and restaurant crowd did not take much note of the article, probably because few of them bought newspapers anymore. The article, however, hit the local and state birder community with a bang, and provided some very contentious discussions at early evening cocktail parties. Did the Yuma fly to Florida or did some Neanderthal from the West cold-heartedly let his pet lose? It was time to hit the swamps with cameras and binoculars. The new energy that swept through the birder community added years to some of their lives. It had been at least twenty years since an unusual bird species had last been seen in South Florida - a blue-throated piping guan. Only a single guan was ever seen, and its origin still remains a mystery, and was still a good topic at cocktail parties.

Emily, being young, did not read the newspapers, and the article did not materialize on her cell phone or computer. Carla from Wind Blades Inc had a mother who wintered in Vero Beach, and told Carla about the Yuma article.

Carla called Emily about getting some newer high-quality surveys of the land. At the end of the conversation, Carla said, “Did you see the article about that rare bird that was found in west Delray?”

“No.” Her stomach muscles clenched.

“I don’t know if it was found near your land or not. The article didn’t give an exact location. Hopefully it won’t cause any problems if we buy your lot.”

“Weird animals turn up all the time down here. They are almost always someone’s escaped pet. We have some strange pet owners in Florida. What paper did you see the article in?”

“The Palm Beach Post”

“I’ll have to read it.”

“Yea, we’ll probably call the reporter to see if they have any more info on it. Talk to you later.”

How did the newspaper find out about the bird? Maybe she had gotten such a good price on the property because the sellers had known about endangered birds being there. They wanted to unload the land before the government found out. Could she sue the sellers if this blew up? Was there anything she could do now? Or should she do anything? That might only make matters worse.

* * *

Lucita was sitting at her receptionist desk in the lobby of Enviro Hounds. She liked to read the local police blotter to see if her old boyfriend had been arrested again, and if the DUI arrestees came from wealthy neighborhoods. She had nothing against wealthy people, and even aspired to be one herself someday, but still, she found it amusing. She bought the newspaper to read the blotter a few times a week.

Teddy did not read newspapers, nor did he check out the local police blotter. He got the news off the internet. About once a week he would read

Lucita's newspaper. He only read it while she was reading it. She made a point of giving Teddy a splendid view of her breasts as he stood behind her sharing the paper. Some days were better, depending on what she wore. She tried to remember to wear a professional button-down blouse with a sexy bra when she planned to bring in a newspaper. She could sense this made Teddy particularly uneasy and fuzzy headed. He could barely respond when she mentioned a particular article to him. She speculated that the button-down probably brought back memories of some boarding school English teacher or maybe French teacher, somewhere up in New England.

"Do you mind if I read over your shoulder for a minute Lucita?"

"Only for a minute, and then back to work for you."

She sensed that Teddy loved being ordered around by pretty women. Just playful. Not too assertive. Being domineering would be too much. She enjoyed being domineering.

She had left the top three buttons of her button-down blouse unbuttoned in anticipation of Teddy asking to read the newspaper. Her bra was a slinky, zebra-print pattern from Victoria's Secret. Men went silly when they saw her in it. She loved to watch even the most Alpha men act like mindless zombies when she leaned in close to them. How easy they were to manipulate. Teddy appeared to be fall into a trance faster than most men.

Jenny, a young biologist, watched from the copy room. Lucita could see Jenny. Jenny was not looking at Teddy. She was staring at Lucita's long legs with a faraway look in her eyes, not unlike Teddy's expression. Lucita crossed and re-crossed her legs. She gently rocked the calf of her left leg up and down. *I'd love to get her into a pool somewhere down in South Beach one of these days.* Jenny gently massaged her right thigh, six inches above her knee. She was becoming moist.

"There aren't many good articles on this page," Lucita said. "Ready for me to turn it?"

Silence.

"Earth to Teddy. Are you OK?"

"Uh … Uh … Oh yes … Uh. Uh. I did see two magnificent ones."

"Which ones? … Oh you naughty boy."

"I like the article about the orchid society. I just love the shape of orchids. They remind me of something but I just can't think of what. Those elongated glossy petals …."

Lucita shifted in the chair to give Teddy a different angle. "And what's the other one?"

"Oh my."

"Oh my what?"

"Oh. Uh … the other article. It was about some bird from Nevada someone found in Delray Beach."

She clasped here hands together and stretched them out in front of her, giving Teddy yet another angle. "Oh that feels so good to stretch my back muscles. You should try it Teddy. Come on, just put your hands together, and stretch way out." She stared at him over her shoulder. "You look really stiff. This will loosen you up."

"I am really stiff. That looks really good." He put his hands together and stretched. "Oh yeah."

"I love animals. Look at the interesting feathers on this bird." She was looking at the picture of the Yuma clapper rail. "Do you think they're endangered?"

Teddy was having a difficult time focusing. He finally muttered in a quiet voice, "Yes, yes, they are."

"Oh Teddy. You're so smart."

"Well, I try to keep up on things. Yes, Yumas are very endangered."

No shit. That's what the article says. Boy, do I have this turkey wrapped around my thumb. "It's too bad the bird died. It looks like someone ran it over."

"Hmmm, hope not. What kind of jerk would do that? Probably an accident. Gotta get back to work." With that, Teddy walked back to his office.

I bet you do. I'm still not sure what you really do all day long. But who cares? You just gave me a hefty raise, and I deserved it for providing you with some first-class entertainment every day. Silly man.

Lucita swiveled her chair to face Jenny. "Oh Jenny. I didn't see you there. Come on over. There's a newspaper story here that I think you'd like." Lucita smiled warmly at Jenny and adjusted the top of her blouse.

Jenny said nothing, but slowly walked toward Lucita, with a small smirk on her face.

* * *

Back in his office Teddy's brain got back to normal. He had enjoyed Lucita's mesmerizing powers. And it had been completely healthy and natural. No drugs involved.

He needed a new plan.

Maybe plant more Yumas? I still have some Yumas in my freezer, but Yumas are now old news. Plus, they're dead. Another dead Yuma would look funny. I'll use something else.

How badly would the owner be hurt if the sale fell through? How long would the owner not be able to sell the land if an endangered species was found on the property? A few months? A few years? Forever? Not my problem. He's probably just a rich old guy. Probably a Republican.

Gotta focus.

Lucita's marvelous little breasts kept bouncing into his mind. Mushing it all up. Turning it into jello.

Plotting and More Troubles

Carla is going to back out of the deal. Her boss doesn't like it. I can sense it. I need relief.

Emily had a date with her boyfriend in South Beach. It was Friday night. She made the trip in a little over an hour, and met him at Cleo's restaurant.

She had met Ricardo in college during her senior year, and they both graduated at the same time. He worked in Miami as a salesperson for a company that catered food for corporate events. She enjoyed the energy of Miami, the Latino atmosphere and people. The Delray area did not the same international population as Miami. Delray was populated mostly by white and black Americans.

Emily walked into Cleo's and looked for Ricardo. He had texted her that he was already at the bar. The smell of Lebanese food immediately made her hungry, and the large painting of Cleopatra staring into her eyes made her feel like she had entered a more exotic world. An oasis from the stress.

"Hey. I'm ready for a strong drink after that drive. What are you having? How are you?" Emily said.

"One of their specialty drinks. It's really good. It's got gin and a cucumber liqueur and a few other things in it. They put some super fine sugar around the rim. I forget the name, but it's on the menu. Here, try a sip."

"Wow. That's really good. I might have to have one. Their specialty drinks are usually pretty pricey."

"Yeah. $13 but I'll get it. You had to pay for parking and gas to get here. How was the traffic?"

"Heavy, but not too bad. Normal for a Friday night." She read the menu and ordered her drink.

"You seem more stressed than normal," Ricardo said.

"Yea. I am. I'm worried about the sale of the lot to that wind blade company. A few things happened this week that could become a big problem. Not a problem yet but it has potential. Plus the first payments on the mortgage will come due soon, and I don't have enough savings to pay it for long. I need to sell the lot, get rid of the debt, make a nice profit. It's like all or nothing - bankruptcy with a hit to my parents. Or a nice profit. Nothing in between."

"You really rolled the dice when you bought it. But you'd be bored without a little something going on on the side beside your office job. I know you."

"Yea, and my mermaid company is teetering on the edge."

"I really like those mermaids. The look in their eyes reminds me of you."

"So what happened? Why the stress?"

"You're right. I would be a little bored without some stress, but I'm hitting the high end of my stress meter right now."

"A little fun with some straps might make you feel better." He flicked his eye-brows slightly, and gave a sheepish smile.

She smiled back. "Oh, you'd like that wouldn't you? I have something special planned for you later. I hope the hotel room has sturdy bed-posts."

"Yea, I made a mess of that last place."

They sat and watched the crowd. Emily told him about finding the bird.

Ricardo said, "The bird issue sounds like it will die off. The competing land though could be a big problem. I wonder if there is anything you could do about it."

"I could drop the price, but I don't want to do that. If I could get hold of some money, then I could cover the mortgage for a longer time if the sale gets delayed. I'd have less pressure to drop the price. I could wait out the other seller."

They sipped their drinks. The bar and in the restaurant were were packed with well-dressed people mostly between the ages of 25 to 40. They appeared to be mostly local business people, professionals, and only a few tourists.

"How much more money do you need every month?" Ricardo said.

"Well the mortgage is about $2,000 per month. I have some savings to help pay it. But only for awhile. I need to keep an emergency cushion. If I could bring in about $1,000 more a month, then with my savings I could last about 5 months longer past the date I had planned to close on."

"Man. That's tough. About $400 more per week."

"No. $500 per week."

"There are 4.3 weeks in a month. Not 4."

"Yea, yea. I know. Somewhere between $400 and $500. Either way, it's just an estimate, and either way it's a problem."

They took another sip and watched the action around the bar.

"Could you get more hours from your boss?" Ricardo asked.

"No. He doesn't really need any more hours from me. The work is pretty steady."

"Mermaid LLC is probably not throwing any money off yet I assume?"

"No. I already told you. I still have to pump a little money in every month."

"Oh, yea ... Do you have you any ideas?"

"Well. I thought about how I used to get a little extra money in college but I never enjoyed that, and when I think about it, I really hate that I did it. But it did bring in good money. I can't say it was easy or risk free."

"No," he said. "Neither easy or risk free. Try to think of something else. A part-time job at Panera Bread."

"That would suck Ricardo. Really boring. Obnoxious, demanding, fat middle-aged women."

"No they're not. The people at Panera are really nice. You eat there all the time."

"Yea. I know."

They watched the bartender do a little Latino dance as he shook the cocktail shaker.

"You can do that on me anytime you want," Emily said.

"Mmm ... mmm. I can do that and more if you want."

"I know you can." She watched the bartender's hips gyrate. "I bet they make debit card scanners better now. You can buy them off the internet. I installed one at that little convenience store that one time in Hollywood, and was able to get about $1,700 before they canceled the card."

"The scanners might be better, but the store owners know the scam better now. They've all installed better security cameras. Plus you're really stealing from actual people, not banks."

"Yea, I'm trying to be a better person. But a lot of those people are screwing us with food stamp scams and that type of thing. Scum."

"Oh come on, there can't be too many of them around."

"You never know. I hear stories. Also all those middle-aged people making false social security disability claims. Ass-holes. They are stealing from us. They're stealing from all young people. We won't be able to retire because those baby-boomer, fat turds are stealing money from social security so they can sit around all day, drink beer, take pain killers and watch the 'Real Wives of East Podunk, Nowhere.' Those stupid liberal judges let them get away with it."

"That baby-boomer generation - some of them can be real pricks. Holier than thou. It's really annoying when they say things like, 'Oh you young people don't work hard enough. You're too self-centered.' Then they say, 'Save me. Save me. I have no money for retirement. I need my pain-killers. I need my $50 of lottery tickets every week.' It is discouraging, especially since the government doesn't seem to do anything about the fake disability claims. It's like the government doesn't care about our generation's future. Our generation has just given up on social security. Our heads are in the sand. So we keep voting for those Democrat and Republican idiots."

Emily played with her cocktail stirrer. "I heard that there's a social security judge in Alabama or Arkansas who gives people social security just because they don't have a college degree. He says that's a disability. Shit - why bother going to college? That judge is a liberal piece of shit. He doesn't care about us. That judge, the government, penalizes you if you go to college, and then you also have huge debt. At the same time our elitist leaders tell us we should all go to college in order to compete in the work world. Many of my friends who didn't go to college have better jobs than the ones who went to college. My faith in those so called leaders has really taken a nose-dive. I used to really trust them."

"And most colleges are rip-offs - $65,000 a year. For what? And they're almost all run by liberal Democrats, from the administration to the professors. They're why we have huge student debts. Not because of the student loan companies and the banks. Plus the professors are so intolerant. They shut conservative students and ideas down. Hypocrites and pricks."

"Lynn was a good deal though. They didn't charge too much."

"I agree. A good bang for your buck."

They both leaned back in their bar-stools, and took in the sights.

Ricardo said, "We're beginning to rant. We're supposed to be relaxing or at least planning on how to get money. The debit card scanner is a bad idea. Agreed?"

"Yea, agreed."

They sipped from their drinks again.

"That escort service I worked for in college paid really well, but I hated it," she said.

"Oh come on. Don't even think about that. I'm glad that was before we met."

"Well, I never had to sleep with anybody, but I think it was only a matter of time. At least the guys were all professional and well-groomed. The worst was that rich, middle-aged woman from some town near White Plains, New York. She took me to a dinner party, and then started to paw at me in the hotel elevator later. Her tits were all saggy, and she had this huge mole above her mouth. And she was married - to a man. And had kids. I think she was trying to re-live some lesbo college experience she had. Yuk."

Ricardo watched a beautiful Latino woman sit down across the bar. "That story's gross. You should have introduced her to your friend Sara."

"Sara likes her ladies under 30, pretty and unmarried, to men or women. She's a nice person. ... Well, I only went on five dates at the escort service. The people were all respectful. Even the lady who pawed me. I hear more college girls are doing it today to keep the student debt down. Boy - I hope those college degrees they get are worth it. Anyway, no to that idea. And thanks for not holding what I did against me."

"I'd never do that. Plus, as you know, I have a few little skeletons in my past. Not too bad though."

"Yea. You've been a bad boy." She smiled at him. "Plus, I'm trying to be better. I've been going to church now for about a year. I really like it. It's helped me a lot with some of my problems. I treat people and myself a little better. I'm a lot happier and feel a lot less anxiety."

"I'm glad it's helping. We'll come up with some solution to your money problems. But let's talk about it more tomorrow. I'm hungry. Let's order dinner and talk about something else. Something less serious."

* * *

It was Saturday. Carla was working from her home office, and she called Emily.

"Emily, there've been some new developments with your rival that you should know about. The owner of the other land that we're looking at has sweetened the pot. They have offered to build a cafeteria and a gym on an adjacent lot. They'd give our employees free membership to the gym for one year. Their pitch is that our employees would like the convenience of the cafeteria. They would subsidize the prices of the food."

"Sounds like BS to me," Emily said. "They just want to suck you in. Then when you commit to buying, they'll change their promises in the sales contract."

"We'll have it in a letter of intent."

"They must be some big corporate property investor."

"I can't tell you. You'll probably find out at some point. Look. I really prefer your lot. It has some big advantages over the other lot. My boss likes both lots, and is leaning a little toward the other one. We're not a charity you know. We're not going to buy from you just because we want to help a young business person. We will do what is best for our company. You are still in the running though. Luckily for you, we have narrowed our choices down to just two lots. Originally we started with six."

"Why did you call to tell me that they're offering more stuff?"

"I wanted you to have this new information as soon as possible so you had time to think about it."

"So you want more stuff from me?"

"No, not that I can think of. No. It's nothing like that."

"OK. Thanks, Carla. I appreciate the info. I'll think about it, but I need to hold firm on my price. Maybe there is something else I could do. Anything else I should know?"

"No. Have a good weekend. Talk to you next week."

Carla really wanted to buy from Emily, and not from the other seller. Her boss had ordered her to make the call. None of what Carla had said was true. The other land owner had not offered anything.

Carla had thought about not calling Emily. She had thought about lying to her boss. He was a nasty and vindictive person, though, and would make Carla's life miserable if he found out. Maybe even fire her.

Carla was 45 and saw herself in Emily. Carla had started her own business right out of college. The business had limped along and generated a small profit. Then she had worked for a corporate giant, GE, for about twenty years before moving to her current job.

* * *

Emily was sitting on Ricardo's balcony when she hung up with Carla. She was watching the hustle of Miami traffic and people five stories below. There were a few wispy clouds, and the sun was bright.

You bitch. You and your boss are playing good-guy, bad-guy cop with me. Just like the car dealers do. Squeeze all that you can out of the little guy. You corporate types don't care about anything but your bonuses.

* * *

A turtle would be better than a bird.

Teddy was staring at the boat traffic from his office window. They would be easier to catch. They would be easier to keep in his house. They would be easier for people to find. They would not fly away.

He did some research. No land turtles were classified as 'endangered'. There were some sea turtles that were classified as endangered. There were some land turtles however that were classified as 'threatened', which is less stringent than 'endangered' under the law. He would have loved to have blocked all development on Emily's lot. The publicity for Teddy would have been fantastic. But he thought that 'threatened' would serve his needs.

There were several bird species that were classified as 'endangered' but birds could just fly off the lot. No publicity if the birds flew away. Dead birds would just not be convincing. Snakes and salamanders were too difficult for his staff to 'discover' at the site, which was a shame. There were several snakes and salamanders on the endangered species list. Maybe I could just injure the snakes so my guys can find them. Or catch a bunch of salamanders and break their legs to immobilize them. No - the raccoons and other critters would get them.

My friends and I used to love ripping the claws and legs off crabs and bugs when we were kids. And then watch other crabs or ants eat them. Great memories from my childhood in New England. Where are those boys now? One was the Commissioner of Environmental Protection for a New England state. The other was serving 10 years in jail for selling pain killers to middle school kids in Massachusetts.

He chose the gopher turtle. It was classified as 'threatened' by the State of

Florida. This meant that under the law a land owner could not develop her land before the threatened species was moved. Also, the owner needed to first get a permit to move the turtles.

What a stupid law. The owner should be penalized a lot more than that. The government should make the permitting process so difficult that the owner would just give up. Maybe the Florida conservation permit officials would approve the permits on a reasonable and fair basis. Maybe they gave the permits out too easily, and took bribes from developers. Teddy didn't know. He didn't pay attention to these issues in the local news, and had not grown up in Florida.

Whatever. It didn't matter to him. He wanted publicity, and he would get it whether the land-owner was only temporarily blocked or permanently blocked.

Teddy knew of a man up in Orlando who sold exotic animals. Teddy called him and confirmed that the man could get some gopher turtles. He would have the turtles tomorrow. The next day Teddy drove up to Orlando and bought five turtles. He put them in a large box in his spare bedroom.

The turtles were each about 10 inches long. Some had gray shells and some had tan ones. Their forelimbs were shovel-like for digging, and their hind legs looked like stumps. They ate plants like broadleaf grasses and prickly pear cactus.

Use a dead turtle or a live turtle? The live would be better, but only if his staff would be able to find it. Why take the risk? Dead would probably be good enough.

How to kill one of the turtles? Since killing the crabs in middle school he had not killed any animals, though six months earlier he had run over his neighbor's male cat who was spraying disgusting smells on his back door. *I did like the cat though.*

Smash the turtle's head in with a hammer? No. That would look unnatural. He decided to cut its throat.

He took a turtle out of the box and put it on the floor with some lettuce near its nose. He waited. The head slowly oozed out of the shell. Teddy reached down to grab it. The turtle quickly pulled its head in. Teddy waited 20 minutes, and the head came out again. This time Teddy moved in slowly and then lunged quickly. The turtle was too fast, and the head was back in the shell.

Teddy waited another hour and did not see the head again. Turtles knew how to wait out their adversaries. They were good at it. Teddy did not want to wait.

He got another box and put a turtle in it alone. He put some lettuce in the box. Then he filled a small bowl with water, anti-freeze and a small amount of rat poison. He put the bowl in the box, and went to watch 'The Real Housewives of Marion, Rhode Island' on TV. The action on the show was more salacious than on the 'Real Housewives of LA,'. He was particularly attracted to the wife of the Boston financial company executive, who reminded him of his French teacher from boarding school. The wife would often inspect their 40 foot sailboat at the boat yard. She enjoyed talking to the young, muscular, handsome black man who was lubricating and maintaining the engine. The husband seemed to spend all his time playing platform tennis with his high school friends, and planning for the coming yacht race. His wife would give him a peck on his cheek once in awhile. His face would light up. But then she would quickly leave for the boatyard, with a look of relief on her face.

At 6:00 the next morning the turtle was still alive, but clearly not feeling well. It was moving slowly. Teddy easily caught its head, and punctured its wind pipe with a sharp knife. He then stuck the body in a plastic bag.

It was a Monday morning, and Teddy had texted Sam over the weekend, and told him to stop by the lot on the way to work to try again to look for any Yuma clapper rails. Teddy needed to place the corpse before Sam got there.

* * *

The sky was gray but the sun was close to burning through the haze. As Teddy approached the lot he noticed about five or six cars parked along the street. There were no people. He parked his card and walked onto the main trail. He walked quickly down the trail. He stumbled over a log and fell into a bush, rustling some dead leaves. His face landed next to a pair of green, rubber boots. He got up and stared into the face of a bearded man with round, wired rimmed glasses. The man wore a light green vest with small pockets all over it. His pants were green cargo pants with two large pockets on both sides. There were binoculars hanging from his neck, and he held a camera with a giant zoom lens.

"Are you hurt?" said the man.

"No. I'm fine, thanks. Didn't see that log."

"You look OK. I don't see any scratches on your face. You were moving pretty fast. Are you a power hiker?"

Power hiker? "Yea. I like to get my heart going."

"I don't mean to bother you," the man said. "But is there any chance you could pick another place to hike today? A bunch of my friends are stationed around this property. We're trying to get a picture of a rare bird. Someone found a dead one near here the other day. The other guys and gals are hidden around the area inside bushes and behind logs. You might scare the birds. If you don't mind, that is. We don't want to ruin your hike."

"Oh … OK. Not a problem," Teddy said.

"Are you sure you don't mind? We don't want to be obnoxious."

"No. No. There are some other trails about 5 miles north of here that I'd like to hike anyway."

The man looked through his binoculars toward a noise high in the trees. "There are? I've never heard of those. I'll have to try them out. Sure you're OK? I hope you didn't squash your lunch in that plastic bag. It looks pretty good."

Teddy stared at the bag holding the gopher turtle. "Oh no. It's in a hard container. Thanks. See you later."

As Teddy left the man whispered to Teddy, "We'll only be here a few more days. And then one a week or so."

Why can't everybody be that nice?

Teddy got back to his car, tossed the turtle carcass into the back, and drove off.

* * *

Emily was in her office at work, and her phone rang. It was Carla.

Carla said, "I had one of our local guys drive by the lot the other day. There were people all over the place dressed in camouflage with large cameras. We're getting worried. The other property is looking better and better Emily."

"Crap," Emily said. "Yea, they must be bird watchers. It's really popular down here with all the retirees. I didn't know they were on my property."

"Have they found any Yuma whatever they're called birds?"

"No. I'd know about it if they had. I'll make sure though. I have some friends who hang out with friends of friends of the bird watchers. Plus it would have been in the local newspaper by now. A bird from Nevada around here is really weird and really big news. Kind of like whose going to be in the lead at the local dinner theater."

"Ha. Ha. Retirees. Call me back when you hear back from your bird friends."

Emily hung up. "Shit." She lit a cigarette. "Shit. shit." Not only could she lose the sale, but she might never be able to sell the property if the Yumas were nesting there. She had heard mixed rumors about the state environmental protection staff. Some were reasonable and easy to work with, and they enforced the rules fairly. But some were zealots who if they could would force everyone to live in mud huts and ride horses - everyone but themselves and their friends who would use their fossil fuel powered SUV's to drive around to enforce environmental laws, regulations and whims. Air conditioning for them so they could regulate, but no AC for the general public. The Secretary of State had said air conditioning was more dangerous than Islamic Extremists. As he jetted around the world, maintained his various mansions in Nantucket and elsewhere, and enjoyed his yachts.

Kicking the birders off her property would only get her bad publicity. Besides, they were probably just like her parents - really nice, and having a grand old time. The birders weren't the problem. The birds were. If there really were Yumas there. A bird from Nevada must have been a pet. But who would want a bird like a Yuma as a pet? Better than a boa? Maybe. But not as quiet and easy to take care of. Maybe the other land owner trying to sell to Carla's company had planted the Yuma. But Carla would not have told the other owner the location of Emily's land. Or would she have? No. No motive to do that. Did someone else want the sale blocked. That neighborhood girl, Lisa, had said her father did not want the sale to go through. And he is a biology professor at some local college. He might know how where to get a dead Yuma.

Her hands shook as she pulled the cigarette from her lips. *Why me? If someone planted that bird ... . "Dear God. Please give me guidance, and please help me control my anger ... and grant me forgiveness. Amen."*

* * *

Later that afternoon Emily was still at work and Jerry called her. "Emily, we seem to have a little problem."

"Great. What is it now?"

"Palm Beach Five-and-Dime just canceled their order for 200 of the mermaid cleats."

"Shit. They're a great client."

"Yea. And it gets worse. I called the manufacturer to cancel as soon as the Five-and-Dime canceled. We have a big deposit with them. They said it was too late. They had made the cleats already. And we owe them another $500 above the deposit money they already have."

Emily walked around her office, staring at the ceiling. "Man. I don't have enough extra cash. The money from Palm Beach Five-and-Dime was supposed to cover the short fall."

"Should we stiff the manufacturer?"

"No. That would kill our reputation. Put us out of business."

"Let's just stall picking up the order," Jerry said. "Then we can pay later."

"OK, lets stall ... Jerry, I may need to shut down Mermaid LLC down. It's bleeding me. And the stress is too much along with my other worries."

"You can't do that!" Jerry yelled. "I need this job. You know that. The economy sucks out there. Lots of people are not even counted in the unemployment stats because they've just stopped looked for jobs. I'll be out on the street! The economy has sucked for 7 years - since the 2008 crash!"

"But Jerry, my cash flow is ..."

"You just got greedy when you bought that lot. You wanted to make a fortune. Pigs get slaughtered you know."

"Jerry, maybe we can ..."

He had hung up. She stared at her phone. Hopefully Jerry would not do anything rash. In college he had pulled some hot-head stunts when he had lost his cool. Never got arrested though. But that was just by luck.

What's Your Hand Doing Down There?

A few days passed, and the bird watchers had left the lot.

Teddy had put the turtles in a box in one of the extra bedrooms in his house. He sat at a desk chair looking into the 3 by 4 foot cardboard box that contained the turtles. It was 7:00 in the morning. Each turtle was having a hard time pushing off with one of its legs when it walked.

He had decided to use live turtles this time. Not because he had felt remorse at killing the last one, but it had taken some effort to kill it. Plus, live animals would look much better on TV. He would hold the turtles up for the camera. Maybe the local Fox station would send that hot blond. Why couldn't MSNBC ever get hot women? Maybe Brian Williams, if he survived another missile attack on his helicopter. The local NBC staffers were pretty good though.

He would plant all the turtles. Several turtles would look more natural than one, and provide better publicity. It was unlikely that a pet owner would have owned a lot of turtles.

The turtles had to be partially immobilized so they would not crawl very far. His original plan was to use pliers to push small nails into one foot on each turtle. Then he realized that people would probably notice that the turtles were not moving normally. Nails in turtle feet on multiple turtles would look odd.

So the night before he picked up one of the turtles. The feet were not completely in the shell. He pushed a small nail, more like a pin, into one of its feet. On the next turtle he made small cuts with a box cutter. They were difficult to see, and would get filled with dirt. They'd heal but he was not too concerned. On another turtle's foot he rubbed in a small amount of sulfuric acid. Two small blisters appeared on the foot. He left one turtle healthy.

After dealing with the turtles, he ate, and went out to the bars. He picked up the 40 year old barmaid he had met the same night he had met Brittany. She left at a little before 7:00 that morning. He could smell the delicious scent she had left on him from their morning quickie. But he had no time to take a shower. He put the turtle box in his car, and drove to the lot so that he would get there before Sam.

* * *

When he arrived at the land there were no cars parked on the road. He could see no birders. He'd be quick. He parked the car, got out, and opened the lift-back to get at the box containing the turtles.

It was cool for South Florida. Teddy could hear the loud sound of palm branches rubbing together in the strong breeze. Shadows from the forest swam over his car.

Just as he removed the first turtle from the box, his cell phone rang. He put the turtle down in the back of the car outside the box. The car was a lift-back and so the trunk area was flat with no lip to the outside. It was about the height of Teddy's crotch. As Teddy talked, he shifted sideways, back and forth directly in front of the turtle's face. He smelled like seaweed infused with a little bit of anchovy paste. It was a new and inviting smell to this male Gopher turtle. It was a smell that many human males found intoxicating. The turtle was drawn to the scent, like a dog would have been. He was hungry. Teddy had been a poor provider of food.

The turtle slowly extended its long neck out of its shell. This was not a snapping turtle. Snapping turtles had been known to snip people's fingers off. They are carnivores. A Gopher turtle is not. They are herbivores with strong beaks. They don't lunge like a snapping turtle. The gopher turtle slowly opened its sharp, powerful jaws and moved in for breakfast. Teddy was engrossed in his phone conversation, and was still swaying when the turtle closed its beak. He bit into Teddy's upper thigh, just about two inches from the source of the delicious odor.

Teddy jumped back, yelped, and looked down. The turtle was hanging from his leg.

He said into his phone, "Shit, gotta go. See you later." It was the barmaid telling Teddy what a wonderful time she had had last night.

The pain was not too bad, but bad enough. Teddy gave a muted yelp, and grabbed the turtle and gently wobbled it back and forth a few times. He did not want to yank it as the beak might pull out a chunk of flesh. It let go fairly easily, and Teddy put it in the box. A snapping turtle would have locked its jaws, like a vise. His shorts were made of a light fabric, and the turtle had ripped a small, one inch tear to the right of his crouch. It had broken Teddy's skin with a V-shaped bite mark. A small amount of blood oozed out. There were paper towels in the trunk. Teddy grabbed one, and reached down inside the front of his shorts and pressed the paper towel against the bite to stop the bleeding.

* * *

* * *

On the way to her school bus Lisa liked to walk past Emily's land hoping to see boa constrictors or interesting birds. She wanted to get a picture of a Yuma on her cell phone, and get her name in the local paper.

The street was a long straight South Florida street. She watched a car park on the side of the road about 100 yards in front of her. When she was about twenty feet in front of the car she heard a man yell. Teddy's head and shoulders stuck up above the car.

She approached the front of the car. "Are you OK Mister? I heard you yell." He had already removed the turtle, and was pressing the paper towel against the bite.

"What? Oh ... er ... yea I'm fine."

She continued walking and got to the back of the car.

Teddy's face was red and perspiring, and his hand was down the front of his shorts.

"Gross! You pervert!" She quickly raised her cell phone, and took some quick photos of Teddy. "I'm calling the cops."

"No, no, no. I'm an environmentalist."

"Yea - a perverted environmentalist playing with your little milk-snaky."

"What?" The pain was now sharp.

"You're disgusting." She took more pictures. *My friends will love this.*

Teddy stared down at his hand in his pants, and quickly yanked it out. "Something bit me and I'm just stopping the bleeding."

"Yea. Right. What could have bitten you there? A milk-snake?"

"Here. I'll show you."

"UUUUUGH ... Stop." She quickly walked back about ten feet, and took more pictures. She started to back away further.

"No. See the tear in my shorts? I don't want you to think I'm one of those weird guys."

"Don't come near me mister." The tear and bite mark and the blood became visible. "Yea. I see it. OK. I'm leaving." She paused and turned back. "What bit you? There aren't any animals that bite around here. Plus, that's a weird place to get bitten."

"It bit me at home right before I came here. I was fine when I left my house, but I brushed up against the bumper, and it re-opened the cut. Maybe it's become a little infected."

"What bit you at your home?"

Teddy pushed the paper towel against the bite. "I have a pet black snake. It's gotten pretty big. But it's never bitten me before."

"My friend has a black snake, and it's really friendly. For a snake, that is." She looked past Teddy into the trunk. "What are you doing with that turtle in the back of your car?"

"Oh. I found it down that trail, and was thinking of taking it home."

"But you just pulled up here in the car. I saw you park it. You haven't been down the trail."

"The turtle was on the grass by the side of the road."

"Yea, right. ... Why would you want to take it home?"

"As a pet. I'd probably let it go in a few weeks."

"It's a little strange looking. I've never seen one quite like that around here. I think I saw one like that on a turtle poster at the nature center."

"Yea. It looks pretty unusual."

He picked up the turtle and walked onto the trail. "You know, there really is no point in bringing this home. I'm going to let it go instead. See you later."

"See you later." She ran off.

Teddy then removed the turtles one by one from the box. He carried each turtle a short distance into the trail, about fifty feet, and put them on the ground in a clearing where they would be easily seen.

* * *

After Teddy released the turtles, he drove to Starbucks, bought two coffees, and returned to the lot. Sam was parked in his car. Teddy had told Sam to meet him there. The small rain clouds had blown off over the Atlantic Ocean, and the sun was bright to the east. There was a smell of newly grown vegetation.

"Sorry I'm a little late," Teddy said. "Would you like a coffee?"

"Great. Thanks. Starbucks - how fancy."

"You have your camera?"

"Yea. All set." Sam looked down the trail, and then up into the trees.

"If we don't spot any Yumas in half an hour lets go back to the office, and come back in a few days."

"OK. I'll stay as long as you want. It's a nice day. We're outside. Not in the office." Sam was staring up at the tree tops, smiling.

"Yea, a perk of the job."

"Your shorts are ripped boss."

"Yea. I know. Thanks. I tore them on a piece of metal sticking off a pickup truck at Starbucks."

"Maybe Lucita can sew them for you back at the office. While you wear them."

Teddy laughed. "No, she's a nice young lady. I wouldn't even ask." *Good idea.*

"I'd love to go out on a date with her," Sam said.

"That would be sweet, yea, but don't forget the office policy about dating co-workers. Especially ones who are below you."

"Is that really enforced?"

"Yes. Someone got fired six months before you were hired for violating that policy." Teddy lied. He had never seen it enforced.

"Who was fired?"

"It was a woman making unwanted moves on guess who? … Lucita. Can't tell you her name. Privacy rights and all."

"Man. I wish I had seen that action. How old was she?"

"About 40 and was married with kids." Teddy was getting himself excited with that fantasy. *I would never have fired a woman like that.*

"Wow. Really hot."

Teddy started walking toward the trail opening. "OK. Lets not talk from here on in. Don't want to spook the birds."

They quickly came to where Teddy had planted the turtles. Teddy whispered, "Shhhh. Let's stop here. Stay real quiet. I thought I heard a noise. A chirp."

Sam looked in the trees. He saw a mockingbird.

Teddy said, "Maybe they're on the ground. Like the egrets you see walking in people's yards."

They both looked where Teddy had placed the turtles an hour earlier. There were no turtles. *They couldn't have gone far, I mutilated their feet.*

Sam looked up, and gazed down the trail, away from where Teddy had planted the turtles. "I see something moving." He quietly moved down the trail. Teddy looked for the turtles in the open area, saw small tracks but no turtles, and then followed Sam.

Teddy had stopped and was staring down. A medium sized boa constrictor had half sucked a bird into its mouth. The lower part of the bird was still sticking out of the snake's mouth. The two men were mesmerized as they watched the bird's feet and tail slowly get pulled into the snake's gullet and disappear. Disgusting. A tough world.

Sam said, "I thought those were just in the everglades. Not this far north."

"Yea. Me too. But I read some guy found a fairly big one in Boca on the beach last month. It went after his poodle, but the poodle bit its head off. But only after the owner unwound the snake from the poodle. One pissed off poodle."

"A big poodle?"

"Yea - one of those huge ones. The size of a golden retriever."

"That was a Yuma that the snake just ate," Teddy said. "I'm sure of it."

"Teddy, you don't know what the F you're talking about."

"I know my Yuma butt feathers Sam." Teddy stared at the lump in the middle of the snake. "Maybe we shouldn't go in much further."

"You afraid of boa's?"

"I saw some birds or something walking around back in that open area we just passed," Teddy said. "Lets go back and check it out."

They walked back to the clearing. *Where the heck did those little boogers go? They are here somewhere.* "This is where I saw something moving," Teddy said. "I assume they were birds, but I'm not sure. Don't talk too loudly."

Sam had a worried look. "Do you think there are any more boas in there?"

"Don't worry. They never eat people."

"Yes they do. I read about one that killed a security guard in Indonesia at a park. People just watched the poor guy as the snake squeezed him to death."

"Well, they're bigger in Indonesia."

"No they're not. I've seen them eat alligators in the Everglades on Youtube."

"Well if someone had just unwound the snake off that security guard, he wouldn't have died. I saw people unwind a snake off somebody on Youtube. Looked easy."

"Yea. That was a pretty cool video."

The two men walked into the clearing, separated by about five feet. The clearing was the size of a tennis court. There were a few knee-high shrubs, some grass and some sandy soil. The shadow from the trees vibrated slowly over the ground. It was quiet. Sam heard a quick rustling in the grass, moving away from him, but he saw nothing. He was looking several feet above the ground. Teddy was staring directly at the ground.

"You'll spot the birds better if you look up a little bit."

"Yea, you're right."

"You're scared of being bitten by a snake."

Teddy was following subtle claw marks in the sandy soil on both sides of a thin line. He followed the tracks for about 10 feet. At the end of the thin line was a turtle feeding on some grass.

"Sam, come here. Look at this."

Sam walked over and looked at the turtle. "Look. There are two more over there." He was pointing a short distance straight ahead. One was walking, but very slowly.

"Maybe that's what I had seen moving the grass around," Teddy said.

"Let's look over there. There might be Yumas hiding in those bushes."

They walked twenty feet to the edge of the clearing. Sam saw an egret leisurely pecking into the ground nearby. He took some pictures of it.

"You think that was a Yuma?" Sam said.

"No. Looks a little different, but we can look at your pictures later."

They kept on looking for 15 minutes. "We need to get back to the office," Teddy said. "Let's go look at those turtles again."

"Awwww ... but this is fun Teddy. You just want to get back to read Lucita's newspaper."

Teddy smirked. "What? Err ... I hope so. I want to see if the bird watchers are in the paper again." *I wonder if people have noticed me reading over Lucita's shoulder? Looking down her blouse? Maybe I should stop ... or at least be a little bit more careful. Jenny seems to always be looking at me and Lucita. Maybe we could do a threesome.*

When they got to the turtles the two men both stopped and watched them.

"Turtles are pretty interesting," Sam said. "They don't have to worry about too many animals attacking them. Do you think pythons eat them?"

"Guess not, with that shell and all. They can't be constricted."

"They'd be hard to digest."

"Gators would be hard to digest too, and the boa's eat them."

Teddy was holding some grass in front of a turtle. "I wonder what kind these are. Do you know much about the local turtle's?"

"I know a decent amount. Not sure what kind these are. I don't think I've seen turtles exactly like this around here."

"Take some pictures Sam. We can try to ID them on the internet. Maybe they're rare."

Sam took some pictures as did Teddy with his cell phone.

"I'll do a quick Google search on my phone," Teddy said. He typed in 'gopher turtle', and immediately got a picture of a gopher turtle. He waited a few minutes, and surfed ESPN.com. Then he returned to the turtle site.

"Wow, Sam look at this picture." He handed the phone to Sam.

Sam studied the picture. Then looked at the turtles on the ground. Then looked at the picture again. "They look the same to me. I wonder if there are other species that look like the gopher turtles."

"Not sure. But this is an exact match. They must be gopher turtles. Gimme the phone please. I want to see what it says about gopher turtles."

He read out loud about the turtles.

Then Teddy said, "They're listed as 'threatened' under the law Sammy. Looks like we've hit pay-dirt. We'll need to confirm that they're gophers. Then we'll call the TV stations, the newspapers and post it on the internet on our site."

"OK Teddy. Don't forget to give me some credit. This was a joint effort. I could use a bonus and a promotion."

"Definitely. Take a video with your phone. I'm going to put mine on GPS. Then film me with the turtles holding the GPS so we can prove the turtles were on this land. Take some photos too."

Sam took some videos and photos of Teddy and the turtles. "This is Teddy Ceppedy, the manager of the Enviro Hounds office in Delray Beach, Florida. I'm sitting here at a lot in western Delray Beach surrounded by a small pack of turtles These aren't your garden variety turtles though. These are gopher turtles. Gopher turtles are not normally found this far south in Florida. Maybe global warming has caused them to move south. I don't know.

“These turtles and their habitat must be protected from development. This land is another one of our pristine Palm Beach County empty parcels that a greedy land owner wants to sell to an even more greedy developer for the all mighty dollar. I will be contacting the proper state officials to make sure these turtles and their habitat are not harmed.

“I would like to thank my assistant, Sam Reynolds, for assisting me in locating these precious creatures and in filming this video. Sam, please turn the camera around so you appear in the video.”

Sam did so for a few seconds, and then turned the camera around back onto Teddy who began talking again. “These turtles are an important part of the ecological chain because they provide borrows that are used by other animals, such as black snakes ….” Teddy gave a pedantic monologue about the lives of gopher turtles.

The night before Teddy had memorized language from the Florida Fish and Wildlife Commission website describing the gopher turtles, their habitat and eating habits. He simply regurgitated this to the camera.

Teddy was sitting spread-eagled and was talking up into the camera. As he spoke, the turtle that had bitten him at the car picked up the scent of the barmaid, and decided it smelled more intriguing than the saw grass he was munching on. Sam watched the turtle crawl toward Teddy at a surprisingly rapid pace, especially given that one of its feet or legs looked injured. Teddy was pontificating into the camera about how even the lowly earth warm is critical for the food chain - except where it is considered a pest and an invasive species in the Upper Peninsula of Michigan. Sam pointed at the turtle. Teddy ignored him and kept on talking. Sam watched the turtle’s jaws open a few inches from Teddy.

“Watch out!” Sam said.

Teddy looked down and saw the open beak about to close. “Get away from me you deranged beast!” He rolled backwards, his legs flying into the air.

He stood up. “That was weird. I’m surprised a wild animal would be so bold.”

“Maybe it had never seen a human before and so had no fear. My neighbor’s dog went for my crotch last night. It didn’t bite, just enjoyed the scent. Its tail was wagging about 100 miles an hour.”

“Sounds like she enjoyed herself.”

“I know she did. The ladies all like the Samsters.”

Teddy rolled his eyes. “Stay away from Lucita. She’s mine …. Edit that last part of the video out.”

“I think Jenny wants to make Lucita hers.”

“In your dreams Sam.”

Teddy brushed himself off. Sam put his cell phone away, and put a cover over the camera lens.

“Grab that turtle and we’ll take it back for a definitive ID,” Teddy said.

“Correct me if I’m wrong, but I’m sure handling or moving a threatened species is against the law.”

Teddy said nothing for a moment or two. “No. If you’re saving one or saving its habitat, it’s legal to move an animal.”

“We’re not doing either.”

“We’re doing both in the long run. Also, we work for an environmental non-profit, and so we have more rights than other people. You know … obviously if the environmental protection agency were here, they could move the turtle without getting in trouble.”

“This sounds like Obama telling the wind farm companies that they can kill eagles in order to save them … save them from global warming … er, or climate change. ‘We have to cut your head off so that we can save you.’”

“You’re an idiot. You don’t understand how environmentalism works. You’ll never make the big bucks in the enviro business.”

Sam stared at one of the turtles, then looked up into the trees. “Let’s stay another half an hour and try to spot a Yuma clapper rail. Then we won’t need to touch any of these turtles. I heard the staff at the EPA can be kind of crazy. You know, extremist, nasty. Like little Nazis.”

Teddy laughed. “Yea, they are idiots, but they have a good gig going. High salaries and benefits. Benefits for life. Great pensions. Screw the taxpayers.”

They watched one of the turtles walking toward some grass. Teddy said, “Don’t worry. We have a good reputation. That one there looks good.”

“I don’t know about this Teddy … .”

“Don’t be a fag… uh, a wimp Sam. Just pick it up. No one is watching.”

Sam picked up the turtle, and they walked to their cars.

* * *

Teddy and Sam arrived at their office at the same time, and parked next to each other.

“We need to take the turtle inside,” Sam said. “It can’t sit in the car all day.”

“Yea. Definitely.”

“Can I use that box in the back of your car?”

“Sure.” Teddy opened the lift-back and gave Sam the box.

“Boy Teddy. This smells disgusting. And that looks like snake poop. I don’t want that stinking up my office. What did you have in it?”

“Oh, I was using it to clean out my garage. Yea, don’t take the box inside. Just empty out your waste paper basket and put the turtle in that, and then go ask the building maintenance guy if he has any extra boxes. Don’t forget to move the turtle to the box before the end of the day. The cleaning crew comes in every night.”

"OK. Sounds like a plan. I'll get it some lettuce too."

"Also, email a picture of the turtle over to that bio professor at Florida Atlantic to see if he can identify it. Professor what's-his-name. Drive it over if he wants to see it. Tell him it's kind of urgent. I don't want the lot to be sold before we have a press conference. The old 'greedy land-owner' card, you know."

"The 'greedy land-owner' card never fails. Poor bastard."

"Who gives a shit about him? I'm sure he's loaded. He can just give the land to the land trust and take a tax deduction. My parents do that often. A little piece of their land each year, and take a deduction for much higher than the land's worth. The IRS never figures it out."

As the day progressed the turtle bite on Teddy's leg became sore and started to ooze puss. The anti-bacteria jell Teddy put on did not stop the infection. The soreness in Teddy's leg became worse and worse. He made an appointment to see a doctor at the end of the afternoon.

* * *

The Florida Atlantic biology professor liked to help local environmental non-profits. He called Sam and said, "Yup, those are definitely gopher turtles in the pictures. The photos were really clear. I could see them from a bunch of different angles."

"Thanks professor for taking the time to look at them so quickly. So are you positive they're gopher turtles?

"Oh yea. No question. I did a research project on them two years ago. I know them well."

"I have a live one here if you'd like to get a better look."

"Sure but not a rush since I'm positive from the photos. Bring it over at your convenience, but call first."

"OK, I'll call."

"I won't touch the turtle though. You'll have to hold it for me. It's really illegal to touch threatened species without a permit. Especially for a person in my position, a biology professor, that would look really bad."

"No problem," Sam said. *Teddy's an a-hole. ... Oh shit, It's still in the garbage can.*

* * *

Two people were sneezing, and a third was just staring vacantly at the coffee table in Doctor Schwartz's waiting room. The man did not show any interest in the piles of *Oprah, Golf Digest,* and *Florida Living* magazines sitting on the table. The walls held four framed prints of mountain scenes. There were about

10 empty chairs. Teddy scrolled on his cell phone for about 15 minutes before Doctor Schwartz's assistant called him in.

The assistant took Teddy to a room to wait for the doctor. In the room was a 5 foot long examination table with paper on top, and foot stirrups on the end, two small cabinets, a sink and a print of a Paris street.

Teddy waited 5 minutes before the doctor came in. He told Dr. Schwartz about the infection, and the doctor told him to drop his shorts to the ground.

"You definitely have a problem there," the doctor said. "Did you clean it, and have you put any anti-bacterial cream on it?"

"Yes I cleaned it with soap and water, and put Moro anti-bacterial cream on it."

"Moro usually works really well. Almost all the time. The cut looks like a bite. It's V shaped. How did you get it?"

"Something bit me."

"What bit you?"

"I'm not sure. I was in the woods, and it happened really fast."

"How could you not have seen it?"

"I was walking through thick underbrush, and at times, I couldn't see below my waist."

The doctor put on some latex gloves. "Maybe a sharp stick cut you."

"No. There weren't any sharp sticks nearby."

"Where were you and when did this happen?"

"I was in Hollywood. It was about an hour ago."

The doctor poked the edge of the wound with his finger. "Does this hurt?"

"A little."

"This infection is a lot older than an hour. It looks like you've had this for about twelve hours."

"Maybe it was more than an hour. I don't really remember."

"Well, I can give you another type of cream, that may or may not work, depending on what bit you. It would be really helpful if we knew what kind of animal bit you. There are some bites that require special creams."

Doctor Schwartz looked in the glass cabinet above the counter. "I had a patient last year who had been bitten, and he said that he didn't know what had bitten him. The infection got out of control and we couldn't stop it. I told him that it looked like we would have to cut off his leg below the knee to stop the spread of the infection. Then, miraculously, he remembered what had bitten him. His pet monitor lizard had bitten him. They have nasty bacteria in their saliva that they use to slowly kill their prey. They will bite a large horse, and then move away. They then watch the horse. When the horse eventually dies from the infection, the lizard moves in and eats it. Evolution has given those lizards a deadly bacteria in their saliva. It's not a poison."

Teddy wiped some of the puss off with a tissue. "So this could be dangerous?"

"If it was a mammal that bit you, you'll need to get rabies shots. In fact we may need to do that no matter what, to be safe, because once rabies starts in you, there is no cure. And it might have been a mammal. That's an extremely painful way to die."

"Were you able to stop the infection on the guy with the lizard?"

"Barely. Once we found out what bit him. He almost lost his leg, and he was screaming like a banshee. I wish we had known about the lizard much earlier."

Teddy looked at the ooze. "There probably weren't too many types of animals that could have bitten me. I wasn't anywhere exotic. Just an empty lot in Delray."

"My other patient didn't want me to know what kind of animal bit him because it was illegal for him to own the lizard."

"Did you turn him in to the police or the EPA?"

"No. Doctor - client confidentiality you know. I was just happy we were able to save his leg."

Teddy sat staring at the floor. "I'm pretty sure what bit me was a gopher turtle."

"Pretty sure? That high up, and you were standing?"

"No. I'm sure. It was a gopher turtle. I really don't want to talk about how it happened."

"That's OK. The guys who come in with gerbil problems don't want to talk about that either. I don't care what they like to do for fun. I just want fix them. Nice guys though."

"This isn't like that doctor. I was just hiking in the woods with a friend, and we started horsing around with a turtle we found."

"Yea. OK. Guys do stuff like that. I need to do a little research on the right type of cream for that type of turtle bite. Gopher turtle? That's odd. They usually don't live in South Florida. I'll call a colleague at The University of Miami medical school who specializes in bacterial infections. Please go out to the waiting room, and I might have an answer in about 15 minutes."

Ten minutes later the doctor called Teddy into his office. "Here's a prescription for an anti-bacterial cream that should do the trick. If the swelling hasn't gone down when you wake up tomorrow, give me a call, and my contact gave me a second type of cream. It's a little different."

"Thanks. Is it safe to wait? I don't want to lose my leg."

"No. No. It's safe to wait. The gopher turtle isn't like a monitor lizard. The infection is much slower with the turtle. The lizard evolved to have saliva that would kill its prey. Not the gopher turtle. They are vegetarians. Although my friend didn't have any specific information on gopher turtles bites. They really don't normally bite people since they eat plants. He had a lot of information on snapping turtles as well as other types of turtles and reptile bites. He was pretty sure the cream I gave you should work. He also thought that any infection from a gopher turtle shouldn't be overly dangerous."

"Oh. OK. If there's a problem, I'll call you. Thanks again doctor."

"Good luck. My friend was surprised that a gopher turtle would want to bite you, and could bite you. You must have smelled a little unusual. Hey, these things happen. Good luck."

Hot, Smart and Clever

When Teddy got out of bed the next day the swelling and the pain from the bite had subsided. He put more cream on it, got dressed, ate a bowl of Coco-Krispies, then drove to the office.

Once there he first took a quick look over Lucita's shoulders as she read the paper and then went to Sam's office. The turtle box sat on the floor to the right of Sam's desk. Although the box was small, there was little extra room in the office. The office window provided a small view of The Intercoastal Waterway.

"Did you hear from the bio professor about the turtles?" Teddy said.

"Yes. He said they definitely are gopher turtles. He could tell from the photos. I sent about 20. He also said he would also look at the live turtle we have, and said I can drive it over anytime. If it works with his schedule, I'll drive it over today."

"Good. Better to be safe."

"He said he won't touch it, though, because the gopher turtle is classified as threatened."

"OK."

"You said we could move the turtle without breaking the law. I'm a little worried."

"Don't worry. I'm sure there are exceptions for environmentalist groups like ours. No one else needs to know we even have the turtle."

Sam looked down at the turtle. "Our entire staff and the bio prof know we have the turtle here. In my office. Can we move it to your office?"

"Well … no. I have meetings with outside people, and I don't want them to see it in my office."

"You could move it out before you start the meetings."

"Maybe. Let's talk about getting publicity. For both of us."

"All right, fine. I'll keep the turtle in my office for the time being."

"The most important publicity I want is TV coverage. It would be great if they could film the turtles that are on the lot. We may need to coordinate that.

We should also tell the local newspaper, and they can meet us at the same time the TV shows up. We can put the photos of the turtles on our website simultaneously with the TV broadcast. The TV should get us a lot of hits on the site. I'll call my regional boss right after the news broadcast. Any other ideas?"

"Twitter, Facebook, Tumbler and Pinterest."

"Great. Make sure you don't tell your contacts at that environmental agency in Boynton Beach about this. I don't want them taking the wind out of our sails. I hate those ass-holes. They are going to try to steal our local funding from the rich people in Palm Beach."

"Come on Teddy. There are some nice people over there. We get plenty of money from the Palm Beach crowd without having to worry about the other enviro outfit."

"They're a-holes. I missed out on about $75,000 in donations last year because of them."

* * *

It was early afternoon, and even though there were only a few clouds in the sky, the temperature was cool again, about 75 degrees. There was a slight musky smell in the light breeze from decomposing live oak leaves.

Before the TV crew arrived, Teddy and Sam had located the three gopher turtles that were now living on the lot. They were in the same general location where Teddy had left them. One had move about 100 yards further in. Sam followed its trail, and carried it back to the grassy, open area where the other turtles were.

Teddy and Sam were waiting in their cars when the TV crew arrived, the reporter, Kelly, a camera woman, and an assistant. Teddy had spent many hours watching Kelly on TV. He lusted after the camera woman as well. The newspaper reporter arrived shortly thereafter. Teddy did not lust after her. He did find her mildly distracting though. They all introduced themselves to each other.

I'm really excited. My boss will love this. I'm having a hard time focusing. She looks better in real life than on TV. And that body. My God! Or the camera woman? Or the newspaper reporter? At first no, but then - that naughty librarian look. ... I've got to concentrate - my boss will be watching this.

Kelly said, "Are you OK Teddy? You look a little, well, I don't know, kind of a little mesmerized. It is 'Teddy', right?"

"Errr .... Yes, it's errr, 'Teddy'. Yea. I'm fine. I do environmental stuff every day, and usually that's pretty quiet work. I'm not used to TV spots and newspaper reporters. You do a great job on TV. It's great to finally meet you."

And your tits.

"Thanks. I hope so. You'll do fine. Just stay loose. Think of something pleasant to keep you calm. Let's do a quick practice before we go live."

"Can my assistant Sam join us on camera?"

"Yes. He can stand by your side, and you can introduce him to the camera. He won't have to say anything."

They prepped for a few minutes. Then the camera went live.

"This is Kelly Carrera for Fox News reporting to you from Delray Beach. We are standing on a parcel of land located on the western edge of Delray, and I am with Freddy ... I'm sorry, Teddy Ceppedy, who is the director of the Delray Beach office of the Enviro Hounds, an environmental activist organization."

"Thanks for having me ... on your show Kelly."

"So Teddy, what have you and your co-worker found here?"

"We were here yesterday looking to see if we could spot any Yuma clapper rails. They are extremely rare birds. An article about the birds on this very property appeared in a local newspaper a few days ago. While we were looking for the birds, we found an unusual turtle. The turtles are called gopher turtles. Sam here has a live gopher turtle for your audience to see."

The camera shifted to Sam who bent down and pulled a gopher turtle out of a box. Sam had a big smile as he held the turtle for the camera.

Kelly said, "So this is a gopher turtle. Where did you find it?"

"On the land right behind us. And Sam brought the turtle back to the office so we could get a positive identification. Some local turtle species look very similar to gopher turtles."

"I can see how identifying the correct species could be difficult. So it's OK for people to move these turtles?"

Teddy said, "We at Enviro Hounds have the authority to move them, but if anyone at home finds one, they shouldn't touch it. They should contact the State Fish and Wildlife Department to find out what to do. Anyway, it's a gentle animal. They don't bite, like snapping turtles. They eat grasses and other plants."

"Why are they called gopher turtles?" Kelly said.

"I'm glad you asked that, Kelly. They dig burrows like a gopher does. And that is important for the local ecology since other animals use the burrows as shelter. Local animals like the black snake live in the burrows, and they are important to the food chain. For example, the snakes keep the rodent population down."

"That's fascinating. What else can you tell us about them?"

"Well, they are legally classified as 'threatened', and that's important because it means that the land where they live cannot be developed because that might kill the turtles and it would destroy their habitat."

"I wouldn't want to be the owner of this lot. He might go bankrupt."

Kelly and Teddy both laughed.

Teddy said, "Boy he sure could. I'm glad I work for a non-profit. But seriously, the owner can develop the land, but only after he moves the turtles. But first he must get a permit issued by the state to move the turtles. So he'll just have to spend some time and money going through the correct permitting process."

Kelly said, "And how can you tell this turtle apart from other regular Florida land turtles?"

Teddy said nothing. He stared into the camera, smiling, frozen. Kelly stared at him, coaxing an answer by raising her eye-brows slightly.

Sam said, "Its shape is unique. As well as its coloring."

Kelly moved the microphone to Sam. "How so?"

"A biology professor from Florida Atlantic University confirmed they are gopher turtles."

"How could he tell? What did he look at?"

Teddy said, "Aaahh … I'll get back to you Kelly on exactly how he knew."

Kelly was smiling and switched her gaze back to the camera. "OK. That would be great. Well we have located a few gopher turtles just a short distance down this trail. Let's go take a look."

The camera-woman followed the group to where an assistant was standing, marking the location of the turtles. The camera woman moved her camera onto the turtles. As with most turtles, there was not much action. Two were just sitting there, but their necks were out, and they would move their heads slightly once in a while. A third was munching on some grass.

After about five seconds Kelly said to the camera, "These are our new residents of Delray Beach, gopher turtles. They are fairly rare in northern Florida, and very rare down here in South Florida. Thank you Teddy and Sam for this treat. This is Kelly Carrera for your local Fox News channel. Have a good day."

She lowered her microphone. "That was a good spot. People always love animal stories."

They walked back to the car, and Teddy walked right behind Kelly. "That was interesting," Teddy said. "I've never done a news report. It must be a fun job."

She looked into the forest and ahead on the trail.

He said, "What areas do you cover? Do you go into Miami?"

"Hollywood to Port St. Lucie."

"Maybe we can go out to dinner sometime?"

"I have a boyfriend."

They got to the road, and she got into the van and shut the door.

Teddy and Sam were standing next to their cars. Sam said, "Good try. She was hotter in real life than on TV. … I wish I could have said more."

"Sorry but I just didn't see an opening."

"Yea. I know. But damn, I've never been on TV. I will have to tell my parents to watch."

"See you back at the office."

* * *

Emily was in her apartment in a modest complex in Boca Raton. There were eight three story buildings in the complex, each with twelve units. There were palm trees and palmetto plants bordering the walkways leading to the apartments. Her place had one bedroom, a kitchen and a living room. The kitchen and living room were separated by a counter, with a white linoleum top. The kitchen sink had no dirty dishes sitting in it, and the counter was clean. A large gray cat was sleeping on the light brown couch. Sliding glass doors opened onto a small balcony with two outdoor chairs.

Emily answered her phone. It was Professor Sanchez.

"I saw something on TV that you should know about."

"Thanks. I don't watch the TV news. They lie too much. What's up?"

Professor Sanchez described Kelly Carrera's news report with Teddy. Emily simultaneously pulled it up on the TV station's website and watched it while the professor was on the phone.

"Oh my lord! What the F. ... Freak, freak, freak!" Her cat scurried into the bedroom. Emily was trying not to use the F word since she had started going to church again. Before that she had used the F word at least once in almost every conversation. "Oh crap, crap, shit, shit, shit ... Ahhhhhhh ... damn, damn, damn ... I can't believe this! Why me? Oh my parents are going to be shitting. I'd love to just disappear, but I can't ... my parents ... my future ...."

"Yea, Emily. This looks bad, but you'll find a way out of this. Maybe the bank will re-work the mortgage."

"Ahhhhhhhhhhhhh." Emily found the cat, then scratched its neck while it purred. Her hands were shaking. "Freak. ... Thanks for the call professor. I don't know what I'll do. I don't know. I don't know. Sorry for the tirade. You shouldn't have had to listen to that. Sorry. Bye."

I'm done. I'm done. I'm done. I can't take this pressure. And I love animals so much, and that's what's ruining me. It's not fair. Not their fault, but why on my land? How did I not see the turtles when I inspected the lot? I must have inspected it about ten times. Buying that land was the F'in biggest mistake in my life.

* * *

Professor Sanchez and Doctor Schwartz were neighbors and good friends.

They worked together on local charities. They both liked to mentor college seniors and recent college graduates because it was so difficult to find jobs. Many of their friends' children were having a horrible time finding work after the 2008 real estate and stock market crash.

They were enjoying a cocktail while watching the Florida sunset from Professor Sanchez's balcony at his condo in a high-rise building. Their wives were on the other side of the balcony, chatting and watching the sunset. The condo building was located on the barrier island running north and south along the coast in Boca Raton. The condo was on the seventh floor, and the balcony was both long and wide, with a gray tiled floor and several potted palm trees about five foot high sitting along the sides.

"Are you teaching the same business classes that you taught last semester?" Doctor Schwartz said.

"Some but I dropped two, and added two new ones - international marketing and internet marketing. They should be fun to teach, and I have a good group of students."

"That ex-student of yours who was trying to flip that lot in Delray — are you still helping her?"

"Yes. Definitely. There's not much I need to do on a daily basis. She has a buyer but the sale's not firm. She's working on it. We talk every so often."

"It's great that you're spending your own time helping an ex-student."

Professor Sanchez looked down at a yacht moving slowly by on the waterway, with a loud party going on the stern deck. "She was one of those kids in college who is reckless and out of control, but at the same time you could tell she had a heart of gold. She was really outspoken in class which is what you want as a professor. She tried hard, always did her work, and got OK grades. She was really smart, but had a hard time focusing at times. Still, she had ambition. A real go-getter type."

"I saw something on the evening news that made me think of her. They had a segment that referred to the sale of land that sounded like it was close to her property. It was in west Delray Beach. This local environmentalist guy had found a turtle that is legally classified, as, I think, he called it threatened. They filmed the news segment at the site, and showed a few of the turtles crawling around on the ground. The environmentalist said that because the turtles are classified as threatened, they could seriously slow down any development of that land."

"Oh no. Geez - this could ruin her if that was on her land. Not just financially but emotionally. She's a really volatile person."

A cooing noise came from where their wives were sitting on the other side of the patio. Dr. Schwartz looked over toward the noise. "The odd thing is, I saw a patient in my office the other day who had a run-in with the exact same kind of turtle that was on TV. They're called gopher turtles. He had a fairly bad infection from a bite from a gopher turtle. It was almost the same day as the news report."

"Do you get many cases like that?"

"I've never had one from a gopher turtle. Once a year or so I'll get a snapping turtle bite. I get some minor snake bites. A raccoon once in awhile. Lots of dogs. A monitor lizard once - that was weird. Didn't know they can be so deadly if not treated swiftly and correctly."

The professor took a sip of his cocktail. "I thought gopher turtles were from up north."

"I know. It was odd. The guy definitely acted strange in my office. He said he was bitten an hour earlier. But from the condition of the infection, I could tell it had been about twelve hours since he had been bitten. Also, at first he said he didn't know what had bitten him, so I told him I may not be able to treat him correctly without knowing what had bitten him. Only after I told him that a patient of mine almost lost his leg from an infected lizard bite did he tell me that he had been bitten by a gopher turtle."

"Really?"

"Yes. A gopher turtle. It seemed like he was trying to hide something. His story was jumbled. I asked him how a turtle could have bitten him on the top of his leg. He didn't want to talk about how it happened. My other patient with the monitor lizard bite had been very concerned about my telling the animal control people that he had an illegal animal. I suspect the guy with the turtle bite had the same worry."

The doctor looked over at the two wives whispering and giggling. "Then, watching the TV news made me wonder about my patient. On the TV segment the guest said the gopher turtle doesn't bite. But my patient said he was bitten by a gopher turtle. He was certain it was a gopher turtle because he was scared to death of losing his leg - he wanted to be sure I knew the correct animal so I could get the correct anti-bacterial cream."

He looked again at their wives, and adjusted the waist of his pants.

"Also later in the TV report the environmentalist said that the gopher turtle was very rare in Delray Beach and South Florida in general. There aren't very many, if any, around here. So the gopher turtles being found at the lot and my patient being bitten by one almost on the same day ... well they must have been connected."

"Who was this guy?"

"Sorry. I can't tell you his name because of doctor-client confidentiality. Most likely he was doing something illegal. Maybe not a horrible crime ... handling somewhat endangered turtles. But some environmentalists might go crazy over that. Whatever. It was hard to feel sorry for him. If you watch the news report on the TV station's website, you'll see him and you'll know his name. In the news clip, there are only two men. My patient is the one who does all the talking."

"I guess I can figure that one out. Thanks. I appreciate the information."

"Another cocktail?"

"Yes sir. I love your wife's 'slippery nipples'. Really tasty. Ha, ha."

"I'll have to convince her to make you a 'sex on the beach'. They're just as good." They laughed.

"In exchange *my* wife could make you a 'sex on the beach'."

"I'd like that trade."

"Will we ever grow up?" the doctor said.

"Hope not." More chuckles.

* * *

The mens' wives, Suzie and Dottie, were nearby on the balcony. They were both 42 years old and very attractive. Suzie had strawberry blond hair cut to her neckline. She had a gentle tan and no shortage of freckles. Dottie's hair was blond and also cut to her neckline, and her skin had darkened to a fairly deep tan. They both were dressed in sleeveless tennis tops, and tennis skirts. They played doubles tennis about three times a week with different groups, and this kept them in good shape. They preferred playing with all women, but would play mixed doubles sometimes. They had finished playing in an all womens' match an hour earlier.

Dottie had taken her tennis sneakers off, and was wearing flip flops. She had her legs crossed, and was gently flipping her top foot up and down, with the flip flop dangling loosely from her foot. Suzie was watching Dottie's foot move up and down.

"They do a wonderful job with your feet Dottie. I love the color of your nails."

"They look pretty marvelous, don't they?" She smiled at Suzie.

"Hmmm. They sure do." Suzie took a sip of her drink.

"Did you see Joannie's face when my vibration absorber flew off my tennis racquet and hit her in her face?" Suzie said.

"Yes. She started laughing like crazy, yelling 'I just got slapped in the face by a vibrator'. Ha, ha. That is pretty funny. She always laughs at vibrator jokes, even the ones we've said a hundred times before." They both smiled.

"We all laugh at those jokes. For some reason they never get old. I also always get a kick out of when the pro yells, 'penetrate deep down the middle.'"

"Yea, I often win the point when I penetrate the ball deep down the middle."

"I really like the double-penetration myself."

"Ha. Ha. I know you do. It's great when we do that together. We always win when we do."

"Hmmm. Hmmm. Hmmm. And that's a really satisfying win, to say the least.

Ha. Ha."

"It sure is, sweety. You also love to tell us 'to get well lubed up' before the matches."

"Ha, ha. You need to get well lubed up or that sun will burn you badly."

"No kidding. I love the way the lotion makes the calf and thigh muscles glisten."

Suzie gazed down at Dottie's undulating foot again. "Yummy. Yea. Those jokes are always funny."

"It took me a long time this morning inserting that vibrator in. It kept on popping out. The strings wouldn't hold it. It needs to be bigger and it needs bigger ridges."

"Ha, ha. ... Did you have fun ... trying to put it in?"

"Yes I did. Ha, Ha, Ha."

"I love watching Joannie play. She has such a beautiful stroke. Especially on her forehand."

Dottie rubbed her sore elbow. "Yes. She has a great back swing, and really bends her knees. Her legs are in great shape." *She can probably crush a coconut with those thighs.*

"Oh yea. They're beautiful. So powerful."

"Her new tennis outfit looked really good on her. I love that lime green."

"Oh, yes. I loved it on her. Hmm ... Hmm." They both thought about Joannie's powerful forehand swing, and her racket-head acceleration.

Dottie said, "Boy, did you see the look on her face when you slammed that shot at her when she was at the net?"

"O yea. She had a look of terror. She actually squealed."

"Yes, you were concentrating on the ball. She did have a look of terror, but she also had a little smile."

"Really? She probably liked it."

"Well, her nipples got really hard."

"Yea, I did see that."

"You would."

"Look who's talking."

"And she got really moist."

"Mmm. I did too."

"Yea, me too."

"I think you and I should spend a little more time with Joannie some afternoon."

"Oh yes. What a good idea. That's one reason I like you — you have such a good imagination."

"Oh so do you. And you are like a little badger."

"I try to be."

They both laughed, and sipped their cocktails.

"You have the best 'slippery nipples' Dottie. I love them." Suzie was smiling and looking into Dottie's eyes. "I especially like them when you add a little fresh lime juice."

"You seemed to really enjoy one yesterday after tennis. You slurped it right down. Ha, ha."

"Mmmmm. It was yummy."

"Uuuuu. You're so naughty, Suzie." Dottie gave Suzie's knee a quick squeeze.

"If only the boys knew what fun we after tennis. They'd be aghast."

"Oh, they'd have heart attacks. They'd love it. Believe me. Did you just hear what they were just talking about? Us mixing 'sex on the beach' cocktails for them? Oh come on now."

The men had heard parts of their wives' conversation. Both of the men slowly began to talk less and listen more. Eventually they stopped talking, and stared out at the clouds, listening. Both of their hearts had begun pumping harder, and their brains had entered a semi-dreamlike state.

Suzie said, "Look at those two. They both look like they just had a deep massage from some young, sexy beautiful masseuse."

"Ouuuu … that sounds lovely Suzie. You and I should do that some lazy afternoon. I heard there's a place in Delray that has really hot young things."

"Really? Hmm … hmm. I'd be up for that. You are such a bad influence Dottie."

"Oh, you love it." Dottie squeezed Suzie's knee.

"Ohhhhhhh … . Don't start that now with the boys around. I may not be able to control myself."

"You certainly couldn't control yourself this afternoon. That moan was so loud."

"I couldn't help it."

"Oh, I loved it."

They sipped their drinks and watched the boat traffic below.

Suzie said, "Those two boys of ours over there are just gazing out at the clouds in a happy, pleasant stupor."

"Yes. It's so funny. Like two little puppy dogs."

"Two little puppy dogs that want to be put onto leashes."

"And ordered to beg." They giggled. "They'd like that. But poor boys … we're never going to give them what they want."

"No way. I like to watch mine suffer. I put my tennis outfits on early before I play tennis. He always tries to touch me, and he tells me how beautiful I am. I tell him 'no, you've been a bad boy,' and I slap him away."

"You're so mean."

"So are you. But he loves it. I can see from what happens to his intsy-binsty thing."

"That's disgusting."

"It sure is. It's so gross. Anyway, I know what you do to your poor hubby. I'm not as bad as you."

"I think you're worse, but they both deserve it."

"Oh yes they do. Naughty, naughty men. We can have our fun without them."

"You bet we can."

Suzie yelled over to the men, "Hey, you guys look pretty relaxed over there."

They both turned their heads toward their wives. Professor Sanchez managed to muster, "Yes, yes we are. It must be these 'slippery nipples'. They're so smooth."

The ladies both laughed. "Mmmm ... yes they are," Suzie said. "We both like them too. Especially Dottie. Don't you Dottie?"

Dottie was looking at the men, and gave a big a grin. "Mmmm. Oh yes. I certainly do. Sometimes I can't help thinking about them in the middle of the day when I'm at work. I just can't get them out of my mind." She gave the two men a deep, warm smile.

Both men could only manage to stammer, "Oh, ah, oh."

Suzie said, "Ok you two, time to eat dinner. We want you two to have good energy levels at the dinner table. Participate in the conversation."

The professor said, "Yes, dear." The men quietly followed their wives through the sliding glass doors into the condo, with far-off looks on their faces. The women kept talking.

Dottie said, "Darling, be a good boy and go set the table, and make sure you do a good job."

Suzie squeezed her husband's shoulder. "And you, young man, go pour another round of drinks. Do it right. Not too skimpy on the ice, or else."

Both men scampered away to do their assigned tasks as the ladies stood close to each other, admiring the orange and red sunset, the outsides of their hands lightly touching each other.

* * *

Emily went to meet Professor Sanchez at his office in a small one story building in the middle of the campus at Lynn University.

"Hi Emily," said Sally Gosh the department office manager. "It's so good to see you. It's been a few years. Professor Sanchez tells me you're doing well."

"Mrs. Gosh. It's great to see you too. Boy, coming here brings back some old memories."

"I bet. Mostly good, I hope."

“Yea, all good, except for some minor problems. Hey, but I made it. With flying colors too.”

“Professor Sanchez should be done in a few minutes. So tell me what you’ve been doing since you graduated.”

The two caught up on old times for ten minutes before Professor Sanchez was free. The stacked trays on his desk were loaded with papers, but the rest of the desk was clean. There was a student’s paper in the middle of the desk with a few red markings on it. The window air conditioning unit was emitting a low hum, and there was a slight smell of coffee. The office looked much the same as it had several years earlier, and it gave Emily a sense of security.

“Good morning Professor Sanchez.It’s good to be back here. It brings back a lot of happy memories. And some tense ones too — worrying about getting papers in on time and passing final exams. Your office looks pretty much the same. Cozy as ever.”

“Good morning. Yes. It’s a comfortable office. I like it, and it is cozy. Have a seat. Would you like some coffee?”

“Thanks professor. Black please.”

She sat in a comfortable cushioned green chair opposite his desk. A minute later he came back in with the coffee.

“Thanks.” She took a sip. “That’s good. Nice and strong.”

“I was a little worried about you last time we spoke on the phone. I would have been upset too if I were you. I don’t know if I’ve ever heard anyone so angry. Are you OK now?”

“Yes, thanks. I’m fine. I’ve always had a pretty nasty temper. Little things can flip me out. And the turtle problem is a big thing. I lost it on the phone. Sorry you had to hear it.”

“Glad you’re better. Stress can be a real strain to your health.”

“Yea, I know. I’ve gotten much better at handling it with a little therapy. I’ve strengthened my faith as well, and that has helped a lot. The turtle thing was a really big hit though, and well … I couldn’t quite stop myself from having a meltdown.”

“One way or the other, you’ll get that lot sold. And at a nice profit.”

“Thanks for the confidence.”

“Anyway, I’ve learned some information from a friend of mine that you’ll find interesting. I can’t tell you how I learned about it. I need this conversation to be confidential, OK? I don’t want to be sued for slander. You know how people sue over nothing nowadays. All those young lawyers out there who can’t find job … they’re hungry.”

“Definitely. Confidential. I won’t tell anyone about it.”

“All right. OK. Here’s what I’ve found out. You know that environmentalist that was on the Foxnews clip on the turtles? His name was Teddy Ceppedy.”

“Yes. I’ve watched that clip about 10 times. I know who you mean. … I couldn't figure out why I hadn't found those turtles when I inspected the property. Before I bought the land, I went over it with a fine-tooth comb. Plus I love animals. I always look for them. I never saw any turtles, let alone gopher turtles. I didn't see anything that looked like turtle tracks. I know I walked through that open area where he found the turtles because it's right at the beginning of the trail. There definitely were no turtles when I walked through there."

"It appears that there may be something more to the story than what Teddy said. That he simply stumbled upon the turtles by mistake."

"How so?"

"My friend met Teddy, and they talked about the turtles. This was *before* the Fox News report. My friend said that it looked like Teddy was trying to hide something. At first Teddy didn't want my friend to know details about something that had happened to him."

"I don't understand. How did he know Teddy?"

"I can't tell you."

"OK." *Confidential. That usually means lawyers, doctors or psychologists. I should know.*

"So here's what happened. Teddy and my friend were talking. Teddy said he had an injury. Over the course of their conversation it became important for my friend to know what caused the injury. Teddy said a turtle had bitten him. My friend needed to know what kind of turtle. Teddy eventually told him that a gopher turtle had bitten him."

"Why did your friend need to know what kind of turtle it was?"

"It really doesn't matter to you, right?"

"Yea - I guess not."

"Anyway, my friend thought that Teddy was acting pretty weird. Maybe it was his mannerisms or something else. It looked to my friend like Teddy had been handling gopher turtles, and knew he shouldn't have been. The bite was in an odd location on a person for a turtle bite. Teddy lied to my friend about certain detail when they first started talking. Teddy did not talk about turtles until he had to. He had said the bite had been an hour earlier, but the doctor could tell it had been twelve hours. You add it all up, Teddy was hiding something."

"What a prick."

"Yes. Your choice of words is a little crass. A Machiavellian. A Jerk. An a-hole."

Emily sipped her coffee and smiled. "Now who's being crass? I have never seen gopher turtles on my property. So he was dumping turtles on my property."

"That's what it looks like to me. Or it at least it makes you wonder. Plus both things happened within a day or so of each other — my friend's conversation with Teddy about gopher turtles, and the TV news clip about gopher turtles. Also, gopher turtles are extremely rare in South Florida. What is the chance that Teddy would just stumble across a bunch of gopher turtles while looking for Yuma birds?"

"So why would Teddy want to plant turtles? Maybe he wants to introduce them so they'll be considered an historically natural animal in South Florida."

"Then he should put them in a nature preserve. He'd get great publicity if he put them in a preserve. He'd be taking proactive steps. Not just accidentally stumbling on them on someone's property."

"Maybe the turtles would be considered invasive in South Florida, and so he can't openly put them in a preserve. The turtles are rare down here. That would be ironic. The headline would read 'Crazy environmentalist introducing a nice but invasive turtle to South Florida'."

Professor Sanchez said, "Do you know him? Does he have any reason to hate you?"

"Never met him. I was in the environmental group in college, but that was all students. He had no connection to us. He never came and gave a speech that I know of. Maybe we competed for the same funding and so he hated us. No. That couldn't be it. The school funded us 100 percent."

"I know. Maybe he hates your buyer, and so he wants to block the sale."

"That could be. It would be a little strange though. The buyer's a wind blade company. Environmentalists love wind energy. Maybe Teddy owns stock in a competing wind company. Or maybe he also owns land, and he is trying to sell it to my buyer and my land is competing with his. Maybe he is a bird lover, and hates how wind farms kill thousands of birds every year. Maybe he loves solar energy, and for some reason hates wind energy. Who knows."

"I don't think we'll be able to figure out why he would want to block your sale. And don't forget, we're not 100 percent sure he was, in fact, planting the turtles."

"The circumstantial evidence is pretty strong."

"Yes, I agree."

"Shit. Shit. Shit. I'm screwed. I have no proof against him. It sounds like he's out to get me. Or not me. Just the land sale. He must hate the land sale. God, this could ruin me."

I'll Get That Mother F'er

Emily pulled her car up to the curb in front of a tan ranch house. The surrounding homes were all mid-sized one-story houses in good repair, with neatly landscaped yards. Lisa was sitting on the front steps, and got up and walked down to Emily's car.

"Thanks for meeting me Lisa. How's it going?"

"Good. I'm doing pretty well in school. I don't even mind going. I used to hate it."

"Are you in 9th grade?"

"No. Still 8th. Can't wait to get out of middle school to high school."

"I'm glad you're doing well. I had some rough times at your age, but I worked through it, and liked college a lot. But it was a little rough getting there. High school was a jungle."

"I'm not much younger than you. I might like to do what you do when I get older."

"Well, if we still know each other, I'd be glad to give you some help or some tips. Who knows? Maybe I can hire you."

"That'd be great."

Emily said, "So I told you I wanted to show you a picture of someone to see if you recognize him."

"OK. Just like in 'CSI'. I love that show."

Emily brought up the Enviro Hounds website on her cell phone, and was on the page for their Delray Beach office. Teddy was prominently featured in several photos.

"Oh yea. I know him. I just saw him the other day, and actually talked to him."

"Really? Where did you see him?"

"He was parked next to the main trail leading into your property. I walked around the edge of his car, and he was moaning, and had his hands down the front of his pants! I yelled 'pervert.' Ha, ha, ha. No, it sounds worse than it actually was. He had just been bitten, and he was pressing a rag against the bite to stop the bleeding which was why he had his hand down the front of his pants. He seemed like a nice guy. A little strange, but not too much. He was cute for an older guy."

"What do you mean older? I think he's about 30."

"30 is older. The guys I know are all about 13. And they're almost all jerks."

"I'm 26, and a lot of the guys are still jerks. Some will always be jerks. Probably until they die."

"Yeah. Anyway we talked for a few minutes."

"And I know he did lie to me about one thing. I saw a turtle in the back of his car. He told me he had just found it on your lot, and that he was going to take it home as a pet, or feed it, or something like

that. But he was lying. I had just seen him just pull up in his car. He hadn't gone onto your property. So he had to have brought the turtle with him. He didn't get it from your land."

"Wow, Lisa, you're an angel. Are you 100 percent sure?"

Lisa gave a big smile. "Of course I'm sure."

"I'm going to pay you back. Let me think of something good."

"Don't worry about it. This is fun."

"Maybe an air-boat ride in the Everglades, or something like that." Emily got in her car. "See you later."

"Wait. I forgot." Lisa played around with her cell phone, and handed it to Emily. On the phone screen was a picture of Teddy with a hand down the front of his shorts, sweat beads on his forehead, a panicked look on this face, a turtle sitting in his trunk, and his license plate.

"Holy shit Lisa. This is great."

The photo was clear. It was definitely Teddy. He looked just as he did on his website. Emily's fingers moved like lightning. Then her phone buzzed. She looked at her phone. The photo was now on her phone.

Emily said, "It will be more than an air-boat ride. Bye."

"I'd like the air-boat ride actually. I've never been on one."

* * *

After Emily left Lisa, she drove to Jerry's apartment to brainstorm with Jerry and Brittany about how to increase sales of the mermaid cleats. As she drove she got angrier and angrier about Teddy ruining the sale of her land. When she walked into Jerry's apartment her head was spinning with rage, and she was muttering curses.

"Holy shit, Emily," Brittany said. "What's up with you? Calm down. Calm down."

Emily sat down. She was breathing heavily in strong, short bursts. "I'm going to kill that mother fucker. That mother-fucker is dead meat."

"Come on Emily, stop. Nothing is worth killing anybody over. Calm down. Remember when you got arrested two years ago. That was not a great time for you. Tell me what the problem is."

"This mother-fucking asshole is trying to ruin me. Me and my parents. I don't even know him or why he's doing it. I'm going to get his ass."

"Who are you talking about? What's he doing to you?"

Emily told Brittany and Jerry about what Professor Sanchez and Lisa had told her.

"Shit Emily," Jerry said. "That guy is one big a-hole. I had assumed the turtles had just kind of migrated to your land. I mean with global warming and all."

"Shit Jerry. That makes no sense. What does global warming have to do with it?"

"I don't know. They blame everything on global warming. Even terrorism. I just figured …. "

Emily said, "Yea. Well they are idiots. They're crafty idiots. They're making money off of global warming. Corporate welfare slime-balls."

Emily sat down, still breathing heavily. "Check out this picture the girl sent me. It's the guy who planted the gopher turtles."

She handed them her cell phone with the photo of Teddy with his hands down his shorts.

Brittany squealed. "That's the a-hole who slept with me and never called me back. What a dick-head."

Emily said, "You've got to be kidding me."

"No. That's him. No doubt about it."

Emily sat there mumbling to herself. "I'm going to be ruined. Bankrupt. All because of that mother fucker!"

Brittany said, "Emily. Don't start again. Keep calm."

"I'm going to get him right now! I know where he works." She walked to the front door, grabbed the baseball bat leaning against the wall and walked out.

Jerry and Brittany looked at each other. "Oh shit," Jerry said. "You need to stop her."

"Me? Why me?"

"You're closer to her. She listens to you more than me."

"Yea. OK." Brittany ran out, and caught up to Emily as Emily was getting in her car. Brittany jumped into the passenger seat.

"OK, Emily. I'm not going to try to stop you. I know you won't listen to me. But lets be smart about this. Don't make it worse. You want to get him. I understand that. But do it in a smart way. You don't want to make it worse for yourself. It's l like the soccer player who hits a guy because the guy hit him first. But the ref only sees the second hit and throws the innocent guy out of the game. Remember Zidane and the head butt on that Italian jerk?"

"What the hell are you talking about Brittany? I don't care what Zidane did."

She sped out of the parking lot. Brittany continued to work on Emily as they drove toward Teddy's office. By the time they arrived, Emily had calmed down, and was thinking logically. They parked on the street with a clear view of the parking lot.

Emily said, "Thanks Brittany, I'm thinking clearly now. Let's get that motherfucker. You must want to get him too."

"Not really. He's just your standard scum-ball to me. Not worth my time. But I'll admit — I'd love to see you get him. But only if you don't hurt yourself at the same time."

"Let's come up with a plan. Maybe we'll do it now. Maybe later. But first we need a strategy."

They talked for about five minutes. They watched a man come out of the front door of the building. "That's him!" Brittany said.

They watched him get in his car and drive onto the street. Emily followed a few cars behind, hoping not to lose him at a red light. He drove north on U.S. 1 for five minutes and then turned onto a side street and into a residential area. He pulled into a driveway next to a small ranch house. They parked across the street.

Emily said, "This is Mark Lorich's house. Or it used to be."

"Yea. I went to a party here in college. He worked in some insurance office. He used to sell coke. Not a lot. Just small-time."

"Really. I wish I had known. Did Teddy do coke with you?"

Brittany said, "He offered it to me. I said I wasn't interested and he put it away. He said he didn't like it, but kept it around for special guests like me. As soon as he said that I should have walked out. But I was horny. He was really good in bed. Really into it, if you know what I mean."

"All guys are. Especially at that age. They'll do it with a cantaloupe if that's all they can get."

"You're right. But he was, well, more into it than your average horny 28 year old."

Teddy walked to the front door and rang the bell. The door opened.

"That's Mark," Brittany said. "He still looks the same. Pretty good. Most guys start getting a little paunchy at that age."

Teddy went in. "Give me the thin screw driver in the glove compartment," Emily said.

She got out of the car with the screw driver jammed in her back pocket. She was holding the baseball bat. She walked up to the back of Teddy's car and gently swung the bat hitting the red brake light cover and cracking it. She looked around, and then pushed the screw driver into the crack. She removed the screwdriver and walked back to her car and got in. Then she moved the car a few houses away.

"Broken brake light. How careless of him." Emily smiled at Brittany.

Teddy was in the house less than 10 minutes. He came out and drove off in his car. Emily followed from about 50 feet back.

She dialed a number on her phone. "Hey Jorge, it's me, Emily."

"What do you want?"

"A small favor. You owe me, you know."

"It better be small."

"It is, and it will help you. It will give you one more arrest to show your boss."

"What is it?"

"Are you on duty?"

"Yes."

"Are you in your squad car or whatever you call it?"

"I call it a cop car."

"Are you close to Glades Rd. and Military Trail?

"Close enough."

"I just saw a guy buy some drugs, coke probably. He's driving south on Military Trail in a red Subaru. His left brake light is broken. I believe you can stop him for that. At least that's what they taught me in my criminal justice class."

"So what's it to you? Why do you care about this guy?"

Emily pressed on the accelerator. "I don't like him. He's done some really bad things to me and to a friend of mine."

"I'm not going to arrest your boyfriend because he dumped you."

"No Jorge. That's not it. I've never even talked to this guy. He's done something that will cause me financial ruin. Something illegal by the way. But not in your specialties of drug sales, breach of peace, burglaries."

"OK. Yea, I can stop him for a broken brake light. Do I need to worry about this guy?"

Emily quickly moved from the left to the middle lane, accelerating slightly. "No. He's harmless. Probably doesn't even own a gun. He runs some environmental non-profit. They all hate guns and the NRA."

"Most of them."

"I know this guy. Believe me. He has a good job. He'd get fired if he gave a police officer a hard time. He doesn't even use coke, except to get down girls' pants."

"I can relate to that."

Emily said, "I bet you can. I see you in my rear view mirror. I'm in a black Civic with tinted windows. He's four cars in front of me in a red Subaru."

The cruiser pulled directly behind Emily.

"I'm right in front of you."

"OK. I see the red Subaru."

The traffic was heavy. There were two lanes in each direction, and left-hand turning lanes every 50 yards. Teddy, Emily and the police cruiser were now in the right lane. Teddy moved to the left lane.

Emily said to Jorge, "He'll go straight to get to his office."

"OK. There are two red Subarus up there."

"He's in the left lane now."

"They both are."

"It's the left brake light that doesn't work."

"I can't see the brake lights from here."

"OK. His office is straight ahead."

At the next light one of the Subarus got into the left turn lane and turned left at the light, its left brake light not working. Emily was able to quickly move to the left lane, and then, the left turn lane. But Jorge was blocked in on the right lane. Emily followed the red Subaru that had turned left. Jorge saw that the red Subaru in front of him had two working brake lights. Jorge turned on the flashing lights on the top of his cruiser and his siren. The traffic slowed down but kept moving. The drivers wanted to clear a path for the cruiser, but they were not sure where Jorge planned to go. There were a few 80 year-olds driving large Lincolns and Cadillacs who did not hear the sirens at all nor see the lights. Eventually Jorge was able to pull a U-turn on and go back to the street Emily had taken to follow Teddy.

Emily called Jorge on his cell. "I'm still following him."

"That was a shit-show."

"Who cares? You're a cop. You guys pull that crap at intersections all the time."

"I had wanted an easy day. Some old lady in a BMW gave me the finger."

"You should have pistol whipped her." Emily laughed.

"I've just been through sensitivity training, and I no longer have the urge to do that."

"I bet you still do."

"Do what?"

"Have the urge."

"I have the urge to pistol whip you."

Teddy started to slow down, and he put on his right hand blinker. Emily followed. It was a country club and Teddy was now driving into the parking lot. There was a guard at the entrance. The guard said to Emily, "What are you here for?"

"We're with the guy who just drove in in the red Subaru."

"For the charity award ceremony?"

"Yes."

"OK. Have a good time."

Emily saw Teddy park, and she parked a short distance away. She and Brittany sat in the car as Teddy walked into the main building. She called Jorge and told him where they were.

Jorge said, "He's parked. He's parked on private property. He's not in the car. I can't stop him for a broken brake light now."

"Can you wait for him to leave?"

"No way honey, not for lots of reasons. Not the least of which is my boss has a way of finding out if I'm doing what I'm supposed to be doing."

"I'm glad to hear that the police department is so well managed. Too bad you screwed up back in that traffic. You still owe me."

"We're even after today."

"You still owe me." She hung up.

Emily and Brittany smiled and waived at the guard as they drove out of the parking garage.

"What does the cop owe you for?" Brittany said.

"Nothing really."

"Oh come on Emily. I tell you everything."

"He and another cop and their wives were running a call-girl operation out of the apartment building I used to live in in Boca. I had figured out what they were doing. I took some incriminating videos of the guys who would go there, and also got some documentation I pulled out of the trash implicating Jorge. Anyway, I saw some guys watching from a van, and I warned Jorge. So he was not there when the police raided the place. So he owes me. And he knows I have the videos and the documentation."

"God, Emily. I thought I was one of your best friends, and uh, well, I thought you would have told me about something like that when it happened."

"Yea. Sometimes I keep secrets even from my best friends. I don't know why. I just can't help it. I still keep a lot of secrets from my parents. For no good reason."

"Man Emily. They're so nice too. You shouldn't do that to them."

"I know."

"At least you've calmed down."

Emily hit the accelerator. "That was a lot of fun. Almost caught that jerk."

"Yea. That was great."

They drove south on A1A with dance music pounding, laughing and watching the palm tree fronds swaying in the strong wind.

* * *

* * *

The beach bar in Deerfield Beach had an unobstructed view of the Atlantic Ocean and the long fishing jetty that stuck far out into the ocean. The sky was gray and there was a slight drizzle. The surf was gentle and soothing as it rolled up onto the beach. Four of the twelve tables in the restaurant were occupied by customers. Emily and Brittany sat down at a table that was secluded from the other customers. It was 12:30 in the afternoon. They each ordered lunch and water.

"That was fun yesterday, chasing Teddy," Emily said.

"Yea. I had a great time."

They stared out onto the ocean, and Brittany said, "I love looking out at the water on rainy days. It's so relaxing."

The ocean was a dark gray, and the rain drops made small circles on the surface.

Emily pulled out her cell phone, hit a few icons, and handed it to Brittany. "This is that picture I showed you yesterday. Isn't it great?"

"Ha, ha, ha. That dick-head. I can't believe this picture. His hands down his pants, and that silly look on his face. Playing with his wanker. Can I send a copy to my phone? I can have a lot of fun with that photo."

"No. I might need the photo, and I don't want you sending it around screwing things up."

"He looks like he's having fun. Fantasizing about me I bet."

"Or his high school English teacher."

"Or his dog."

"Hope that bite really hurt."

"Oh well. He wasn't too much of a pervert with me. Just an a-hole. Only a dick wouldn't return texts from a girl he had just slept with."

"Yup. There are plenty of dicks out there. I count my blessings that I found Ricardo."

"I'm jealous. I wish I had a Ricardo. Does he have any friends?"

"Maybe. I'll talk to him about that."

Their food arrived and they started eating.

"I've never seen a guy go so wild over sex before. He just loved it. If we had dated, I would have had him eating out of my hand. And I know that type — he would have loved it. I would have had great sex for myself and an obedient boyfriend. What could be better?"

"I wonder if you could still get him to eat out of your hands."

"Why? What are you thinking about?"

"If you could seduce him, and take some photos, or get some type of blackmail evidence against him, maybe I could force him to do what I want."

"I'd love to seduce him again. Boy ... what great sex. Then I'd love to abuse him. But it wouldn't work. He wants nothing to do with me. Not only does he not return my texts, but he wouldn't even talk to me when I saw him in a bar recently. He said 'hello' when I said 'hi' to him, and then he turned away. Arrogant and rude."

"Oh. That blows. He's weak. Easy pickings. ... He's ruining my life."

They ate more of their lunch, and stared out at the Atlantic.

Brittany smiled. "I know a way to get him. And this will be fun."

"Oh yea, what are you thinking?"

"I have this friend, Sally. She is absolutely drop-dead gorgeous. When she walks into a room, all the men turn their heads, even the 50 year old guys. It's like she could lead any of them around by their pricks, make them bark like dogs, and they would come back for more.

"But the best part is she loves to play with them. Really play with them. She gets a kick out of abusing them. Just the jerks though. The guys who are asking for it. She really enjoys it, if you know what I mean. She would probably love to help you out."

"Call her up. She sounds perfect."

Brittany tried Sally, but there was no answer. "I'll have to get hold of her later. I'll get back to you. Just so you know, you'll probably have to pay her. She likes abusing a-holes, but she likes money even more."

"That's a problem. I'm really strapped for cash right now. I don't want to have to choose between Mermaid LLC and the land."

"You better choose Mermaid LLC. I need that job."

"Let's get hold of Sally first, and then I'll worry about the money."

"I'll talk to her, and get back to you." Brittany took a bite of here sandwich. "Man, the rain on the ocean is so beautiful. The way it flattens out the waves."

The Dominatrix Gets Her Due

"Let me at this prick," Sally said.

Emily, Sally and Brittany were sitting on a bench at South Beach Park in Boca Raton, overlooking the Atlantic Ocean. The four feet high surf was crashing 20 feet out from the beach, then it moved up the gentle slope with a rumble as it tossed the sand and a few small shells before receding back into the ocean. There was a slight smell of seaweed, and the gulls squealed and cawed overhead. The three ladies watched the quickly moving legs of the sandpipers running between the foam.

Both Emily and Brittany told Sally their Teddy stories.

Sally said, "He deserves it. Brown University grad. He must be a rich trust fund boy. A lot of environmentalists are. The volunteers usually aren't. They're usually nice animal lovers. Brown is some rich preppy boy college in Ohio I think."

Emily said, "Close. But it's in Rhode Island. Where 'The Drunken Clam' is, the one in 'Family Guy.' It's not in the Southeast Conference. They're good at sailing, squash, croquet. That sort of high brow thing."

"He'll be sucking on my croquet mallet by the time I get through with him," Sally said. "All lubed up. And begging for more. This will be fun."

Emily smiled and winked at Brittany.

Sally was just as Brittany had described. Gorgeous. Six feet tall. Straight, blond hair to her shoulders. Slight tan. Perfect complexion. 140 pounds. Perfectly proportioned figure. Long legs. She had been a star on the Florida State Women's lacrosse team. Strong muscles. Beautiful face. Deep blue eyes.

"So I do my thing with poor old Teddy," Sally said. "He'll love it."

Emily said, "Oh he will. Too much, probably."

"What's your end-game?" Sally said.

"I want him to suffer a little," Brittany said. "But not too bad."

Emily said, "Not me. I really want you to make him suffer really badly, ruin him. Make him your bitch. And I'll need to fix a problem he made for me."

Sally said, "Look no further. That's what I specialize in."

Emily handed Sally a book entitled *Dominatrix 101: The Good Girl's Quick Guide to Dominating Her Man*. "Here's some research material for you. You might get some good ideas out of it. I just got it from Amazon. Never read it. I'm not into that, but it looks pretty entertaining."

"Hah. Yea. I've seen this advertised. Always wanted a copy. Thanks. I probably could have written it in high school."

"Enjoy," Emily said.

"We need to talk money," Sally said. "Even though this is fun and kind of a hobby of mine, I need to get something more tangible out of this. It takes planning, time, money and effort. My fee will be $1,000."

"Whoa. $1,000? I don't have that. How about $500. Even that is a stretch for me."

"No. $1,000. My expertise is like that of a lawyer's. I've spent years working on my technique. Also I know that I have the physical attributes that turn a man's mind into malleable mush. And there's also my time. Time is money. Planning is key. Planning takes lots of time. Then there's the pick up at the bar. Then the time at his apartment — hopefully just a few hours. But you never know. I have two helpers, too. They are awesome at what they do."

"Two helpers?" Emily said.

"Two of my girlfriends. I need wingmen at the bar. Guys are more trusting of women who are in a group. Guys are leery of women by themselves. They worry about psycho women. And they should be."

"$200 now and the balance on completion."

"No. I've been stiffed before."

"I don't have the money. And I don't have time to save it."

Sally said, "I'm the best. I'll have poor Teddy cornered. Imagine the fun we'd all have. You'll dream up some way to get the money."

"Maybe," Emily said. "But I think your fee is high. Especially since you enjoy what you do."

"You're supposed to enjoy what you do," Sally said. "That's what our parents and professors say. Somehow I think they know they're BS'ing us when they say that."

"No doubt," Brittany said.

They ate their lunch, talked about people they knew, and then Sally gave Emily her cell phone number, and left. Emily and Brittany had dessert.

"She is beautiful and a real Amazon," Emily said. "She'd make mince-meat out of Teddy. I wish I had the money. I don't want to take a cash advance against my credit card. Although why not? If I'll have to declare bankruptcy anyway, I would just wipe out the credit card debt in the bankruptcy. But I need that credit card, and if I take a cash advance, I'll probably hit my credit limit soon."

The two women tried to dream up other ways to get at Teddy, but each was either too far fetched, would take too long, or would cost too much. Both of them finished their coffees staring out at the swells in the Atlantic. A few surfers rode the small waves.

"Thanks Brittany for your ideas."

"Don't get down on yourself Emily. You'll come up with something. A-holes don't always win."

Emily paid the bill, and the two of them left the restaurant.

* * *

Emily went to her apartment after leaving the restaurant, and sat on her small balcony. Palm tree fronds almost touched the railing. They hung still in the breeze-less evening. She lit a cigarette, and dialed Sally on her phone.

"Hi Sally. Suppose I pay you more, but nothing up front? And you get paid out of the proceeds from the sale of my land?"

"Don't like it. Suppose you don't sell the land?"

"I'm sure I'll sell it."

"Maybe not. Your buyer might walk. Then I'll never get paid."

Emily took a puff of her cigarette. "I'll sell it to someone else."

"That could take years."

"You can charge me more. It would be worth the risk."

"How much?"

"$2,000."

Sally said, "No. Not enough. In your sale, do you have a sales contract and are there contingency clauses where the buyer can back out?"

"Yes and yes." Emily explained parts of the contract to Sally but did not disclose the price. "The sale has been reported in the The Palm Beach Post. Check it out online."

Sally said, "I want $4,000."

Emily looked down at someone walking their dog. "That's robbery. $3,000. That's triple your regular fee."

"$3,000 it is, but I want $500 up front. The enjoyment I get is my fringe benefit."

"Payment only upon sale? And $500 up front is fine. The $500 goes against the $3,000."

"Agreed," Sally said. "All good."

"You need to do this in two days."

"No problem."

"I'll drive the $500 over now. Will you be home?"

"Yes. Now is good. Here's my address."

* * *

*   *   *

The cocktails were expensive, as was the decor of the room. A 30-foot long piece of light brown driftwood that bowed out in the middle formed the bar. The top of the wood was painted with polyurethane. Water gurgled down a vertical waterfall behind the bar. The ceiling was thirty feet high in places, and twenty feet high in others where five foot wide sections crossed the room to give variety. Giant, dim, art deco light fixtures hung from the ceiling.

Jamal, the bartender, had a nature show on TV. The clientele would change the channel to sports soon. Three lionesses had surrounded a large, powerful male wildebeest that had separated from the herd. The wildebeest was putting up a good fight, but the lionesses were relentless, and were slowly wearing the bull down. The alpha lioness had perched herself on the bull's neck and she was working her way to the throat. A male lion was lying 50 yards away, watching and cleaning its front paws with its tongue.

Teddy sat down at the bar and watched the lionesses weakening the bull.

"Hi Teddy. How are you?"

"Good Jamal. And you?"

"Well. What would you like?"

"A 'slippery nip …." No, not that. Just had one."

"Ha, ha. You wish you just had one."

"A 'monoloco zombie' please Jamal."

"Where the heck do you learn about these drinks Teddy? You must have a cocktail book at home. No problem. It's a little slow at the bar right now. I'll look it up online."

*   *   *

Sally had recruited Brittany to sit outside Teddy's house in her car. They knew Teddy went out every Thursday night at about 9:00. So Brittany arrived outside his house at 8:15. His car was in the driveway. He drove off at 8:50, and Brittany followed. He parked on the street. She parked and watched him go into the bar. She called Sally.

*   *   *

The alpha lioness had reached the wildebeest's throat, and had clamped tightly on the air-pipe. Another lioness was gnawing on the bull's hind thighs and one was on the bull's back.

Sally and her two friends entered and sat at the bar a few seats from Teddy. Teddy was watching the lionesses. The ladies ordered drinks.

Time is money in all businesses, including Sally's. She was also paying for the drinks. Her friends could suck them down, especially when the drinks were paid for. Cocktails at a high-end bar in Boca Raton cost $13 to $15.

Jeanie and Pam were both 28 years old and were as good looking as Sally. Jeanie had an innocent girl next-door look with auburn hair cut just below her ears. Pam was Africa-American and had a round face, Cleopatra like eyes, full lips, and a round, muscular butt. Jeanie had gone to the University of Florida. Pam had graduated from Lynn University. The three had met while playing in a beach volley ball league. After graduating from college they had all move to the Delray Beach area. All three had worked together before in various schemes to get revenge on ex-boy friends and their friends ex-boyfriends. They were pros and they enjoyed their work.

Jeanie said to Jamal, "I love nature shows. This is a little gruesome for this early in the evening though."

"Yes, it's gruesome," Pam said. "I wonder if the wildebeest will escape."

Jeanie turned to Teddy. "You think the wildebeest will make it?"

"He looks pretty big and strong." He had been staring at the TV, and had heard the ladies sit down, but had not looked at them yet. "I think he'll shake them off." He moved his eyes from the TV to Jeannie, and then to Pam and Sally. *Holy cow. Way out of my league.* "I don't know if it's a wildebeest or a water buffalo," he managed to stammer.

"Oh it's a wildebeest, I'm sure," Pam said.

"I don't know Pam," Jeanie said. "I think it could be either."

Jeanie turned to Teddy. "What do you think?"

Teddy's head was beginning to swirl. "I'll have to go with wildebeest."

"I'm going with water buffalo," Pam said. "Let's see what the announcer says."

They continued to talk. Sally bought him a drink, and then later he bought them drinks.

"So where do you live?" Sally said.

"Just about 10 minutes from here. Close."

"Why don't we go over to your place and have some drinks? The cost adds up here. Between the four of us, each round is about fifty bucks."

"Good idea. I'd love for the three of you to come over."

Teddy gave them his address, and they all left the bar after they finished their drinks.

* * *

Sally pulled her car behind Teddy's in his driveway, and got out. She was wearing a knee-length tan skirt that hugged her figure, but not too tightly. Her blouse was a white button-down, over which she wore a light blue cotton v-neck sweater. She wore brown, low healed shoes. Her hair was in a bun, and she had on black eye-glasses. She looked like a model from a preppy clothing catalog.

Teddy said, “Where are Jeanie and Pam? Are they still coming over?”

“No,” Sally said. “They changed their minds. They have to be at work tomorrow at 8:30, and they said it was getting late. I don’t have to be at work until 10:00, so I can stay out a little longer.”

“That’s too bad they couldn’t make it. You’re brave coming here alone, to a stranger’s house.”

“Ha, ha. You seem pretty normal. At least you did at the bar. If you start getting weird on me, I’ll just run out of the house really fast. You’ll never catch me. Ha, ha. I was a starter on the Florida State women’s lacrosse team you know.”

“That’s impressive. Division I lacrosse. It’s really hard just to make the team, let alone be a starter.”

“That’s right.”

“Lacrosse — you must have some muscle to have played that sport. That’s a real aggressive sport too. Lots of slashing and whacking with those sticks.”

Sally smiled, lifted up an arm, and flexed her bicep. “Yea, I really enjoyed it. Wish I could still play, but there aren’t any female adult leagues or coed leagues. Unlike soccer.”

Sally took a step up onto the walkway leading to the house, and looked down into Tedddy’s eyes. “Aren’t you going to ask me inside?”

“Oh, sorry. Yes. Of course. Come on in.” Teddy led the way into the kitchen.

“So how do you stay in such good shape? Running?”

Sally said, “No, I run only a little. I play a lot of volleyball. Beach and indoor.”

“That’s a great sport.”

“How about you? Did you play any sports?”

“I was on my college sailing team.”

“Did you wear knee pads on the boat? Ha, ha.”

“Knee pads? What for?”

“Just kidding. For crawling around on the deck.”

“Ah … no. No knee pads. No protection needed. Foul weather gear sometimes.”

“How about getting me a drink Teddy? A gin and tonic.”

“Uh … OK. A G and T with a lime wedge?”

She stared around the kitchen. “Yes.”

He made them both drinks.

“Why do you keep a copy of your Brown University diploma on your refrigerator?”

"Happy memories, I guess. I should probably just keep some photos instead."

She took the drink from him. "Whatever works for you. Let's go watch TV."

"How about some music instead?"

"No. I prefer TV."

"Uh, er, OK. Follow me." She was already ahead of him walking into the living room. He followed her. *This one's a piece of work. Maybe I shouldn't have asked her back to the house.* They sat down on the black couch, and Teddy turned on the 70 inch high definition TV. He lit a lavender scented, and turned off the lights. A chambered nautilus sat on a stand on the end table, and there were several framed Ansel Adams photos hanging on the walls.

Teddy said, "What do you want to watch? A movie or a show or sports?"

"Women's tennis."

"How about basketball?"

"No. Women's tennis."

"OK. Sounds like you want women's tennis."

"Yea. I love it. Some of them are hitting their serves at 125 miles per hour. And in doubles they hit it really hard - right at the net person."

"You like that?"

"Yes. Yes I do. Those ladies have incredible reflexes."

"I'll say."

"I bet you like their short skirts Teddy. Sometimes you can see their butt cheeks. Ha, ha."

"Hey, hey. I hadn't noticed. I'll have to look more closely."

"You'll like it. I do. Adds a little zip for your viewing pleasure." She giggled.

Is she a lesbo? Bi?

Five minutes later she said, "Teddy, you make a good gin and tonic. I could use another … please?"

"Can you wait a minute? I still have a few sips left."

She stared into his eyes for a long moment. She had a poker face. Then she smiled, and turned her head back to the tennis match, and said, "I'm enjoying this. These two have some power on both sides, forehand and backhand. Nothing like a strong two-handed backhand."

Teddy finished his cocktail quickly. He got up, took her glass from the table. "I'll be right back."

She did not say anything, nor did she turn her head from the tennis match. She lifted here glass up. Teddy took it and walked to the kitchen.

Teddy made two more G and T's, and returned to the living room. When he walked into the room Sally was no longer sitting on the couch, but leaning against the back it.

Her eyes followed him as he walked across the room. He put her cocktail glass on the coffee table. She stared at him, removed the pin holding her hair in a bun, and shook her head. Her blond hair cascaded down to the top of her shoulders.

Teddy was transfixed by her face, her hair and her eyes. He said nothing.

She looked at the glass, then walked over, picked it up, and took a small sip. "Teddy, I know what you want."

"What do you mean?"

"You know that I know what you want."

Teddy was looking at her. "I don't really want anything else. I'm happy just having a drink, hanging out with you and watching tennis."

"You probably are pretty happy just watching tennis with me. But I know you want more. I can tell from the look in your eyes."

"I'm pretty happy with what I have now."

"You want me Teddy. And you want me badly. Most men want me, but you have a really strong urge. Much more than most men have."

"You are very pretty, and you're quick and fun. Yes, I am attracted to you."

"I bet you easily lose control around pretty women. You keep on looking at my body, and my nice long legs. Go ahead, and look. I kind of like it."

Teddy held his gaze firmly into her eyes, and tried to think of something to say.

"Go ahead and look at my legs. They're really strong looking aren't they. But beautiful. Really beautiful."

Teddy slowly lowered his eyes and looked at her legs, and then back up to her face. "It must be all that volleyball."

"Here's the thing Teddy. We both know what you want. It's no secret. But this is about what *I* want. Not what you want. After you make me happy, then maybe, if you're lucky, I'll make you a little happy too."

"We need to slow down a little here. I like to call the shots, and you've already gone too far. This is my house, and I'm a good host. But we've reached a point where it's time for the host to assert himself, and for you to be a bit more gracious as a guest."

Sally raised herself from the back of the couch, and rose to her full height, slowly walked over to Teddy, and gave him a gentle slap on his face. "No Teddy. You have that backwards. It's time for your guest to assert herself. And for you to be a lot more thankful that I'm spending my precious time with you. You're lucky to be with a woman like me. And I expect you to do what I tell you to do."

"Now look here Sally. I'm a few years older than you. I'm the head of an environmental agency. I run a large office with a lot of people who answer to me. I'm the one who's always in control, both at work and socially. Maybe it's time for you to leave."

Sally smiled, and gave him another light slap across the face. A little harder this time. “I don’t think so. You really don’t want me to leave. I’ll go only after you’ve made me happy. You’d better do a good job. I think you’re going to enjoy this Teddy.”

“Enjoy what?”

She lowered her eyes down to his waist. “I can see you’re already enjoying this.”

“I’m sorry. That’s rude of me.”

“You like being bossed around. Being told what to do.”

She was about the same height as Teddy. She put her hand on top of his head, and gently pushed down. “I want you on your knees Teddy. On your knees. Kneeling in front of me. Remember — this is about me, not you.”

“I’m not getting on my knees.”

“Down on your knees.” Sally smiled at him. “I know you Teddy. You want me so badly you’ll do anything I tell you. You crave me. Down Teddy. Get down on your knees like a good little boy.”

Teddy gave a slight moan. He stared at Sally’s eyes and at her lips. She had on deep red lipstick. She slowly ran her tongue around her already moist lips. He stared at her tongue as it slid over those lips. Those lips, so moist and red. He slowly dropped to his knees, and continued to stare at her face. But now he was staring up as she towered over him. He said nothing.

“Tell me you want me, Teddy. I want to hear it. Tell me you crave me. That you’ll do anything for me. That you’ll do anything that I tell you.”

Teddy’s mind was in a haze. He was unable to say anything. Unable to obey her commands.

“What a bad boy. But I’m going to give you a reward Teddy. For obeying me. For getting down on your knees. But I’m also disappointed in you. You didn’t obey all my commands. You did not answer me.” She shook her head, staring down at him, and grinning. “Tsk. Tsk.”

“Please. I er … Please.”

“Please what? Do you want your reward or do you want your punishment? I can’t quite tell. You’re just down there stammering incoherently. Not making much sense.”

Teddy just stared upwards. His heart was throbbing. His mind was blank.

Sally put her hand under his jaw, and rubbed softly, as he stared up into her face, at her lips. She then stepped back, continuing her stare. “Here is your reward.”

She backed away from him about 5 feet. She slowly unbuttoned her blouse and pulled it off. Then she reached behind her waist and unclipped the hook on her skirt. It fell to the ground.

Teddy stared. Mesmerized. Quiet. Throbbing.

A black leather strap crisscrossed her chest, covering her small breasts. The strap went around the back of her neck, and the two ends connected to the top of the small shorts she had been wearing under her skirt. The shorts were only slightly larger than panties, and made of black, silk-like material. She had changed her shoes to four-inch black high heels with thin straps that climbed to the top of her calves.

Her body was tall, lean, and muscular, but not overly muscular. She looked like an Olympic beach volleyball player. She stared at him, and then slowly walked toward him.

He watched her from his kneeling position, staring at her face. She stopped about a foot away. He dropped his gaze from her face, leveled his head, and looked straight ahead, into her crotch. He could smell her body. His heart was pounding, and his body was tingling.

She grasped the back of his head with her two hands. She pulled his face forward, about a foot from her crotch.

"I want you to make me happy Teddy. Can you do that?"

Teddy's brain was throbbing. He was in a trance — the sight of her crotch, so close, and the wonderful aroma. He felt like he was floating in a hot stream, the currents gently pushing him back and forth.

"Can you Teddy."

"Yes …. I can."

"Teddy. You are a hungry man. A very hungry man. I will give you what you want, but first I get what I want."

Teddy continued to just stare. He finally was able to mutter, "OK."

"I want to hear you say 'Yes Mistress Sally.'"

Silence. Teddy raised his gaze from her thighs to her face.

"'Yes Mistress Sally'. Say it Teddy."

"Yes Mistress Sally."

"Good boy."

"Now lead me to your bedroom."

Teddy started crawling to the bedroom.

"Stand up and walk Teddy. Crawling would take all night."

Teddy got up. He slowly walked to his bedroom, with Sally closely following, carrying her purse.

They entered the bedroom. She said, "Take off your clothes and lie on the bed, on your back."

"Yes Mistress Sally."

"That's good Teddy. You're learning."

He lay down on the bed, wearing only boxer shorts.

She pulled four black leather straps out of her purse.

"Do you know what these are for Teddy?"

"Yes."

"Show me."

He raised his arms over his head, pointing toward the corners of the headboard. He spread his legs a little, pointing toward the corners of the foot board.

She tied his arms and his legs to the bed posts. Next she took out a cell phone, place it on the bureau with the lens aimed at Teddy, and hit record.

Teddy stared. "What … what are you doing?"

"Oh nothing. I need to leave by 1:00 and I set an alarm. Don't you worry your little head."

"Oh. You have to leave?"

"Not now, Teddy. Later."

"Oh."

"Remember, silly boy? I have to be at work in the morning. What am I going to do with you?"

"Oh yes. I remember."

On the other side of the room Sally set up a second cell phone camera. It was also aimed at Teddy.

"Now Teddy it's time for some fun, for me that is. But I can tell you're enjoying this as already." She was staring at his boxer shorts.

"Yes, Mistress Sally, but please don't …."

* * *

Teddy's neighbor, Mrs. Gomez, was walking her six month old baby by Teddy's house. The baby would not sleep. The temperature was in the low 70's, and Teddy had left his windows open for the fresh air. She stopped the stroller to readjust her baby, who was sliding out the front of the stroller feet-first.

She heard a muted whip-like sound come out of Teddy's house. Followed by a low moan. Then another whip sound and a moan. Then a low "Auuuuu." She pulled out her phone to call 911 when she heard a woman's voice, "Have you had enough?" Then a man say, "No. No. Please don't stop, Mistress Sally."

Mrs. Gomez put her phone away and said, "Ha, that Teddy. He's a nice man, but sometimes he brings some strange ladies over to his house."

* * *

Teddy was still lying on the bed, with his eyes partially closed, and with a small, silly grin on his face. Sally's high heels clicked loudly on the tile floor as she walked out of the bedroom door. Teddy stared at her rear-end as it undulated rhythmically in time with her heels. "Where are you going?"

She ignored him.

She went into his kitchen and opened the refrigerator looking for a something to drink. She found a Coke, took it out, and opened the freezer to get some ice. Next to the ice bin were several clear plastic bags. In each was a frozen bird. She went back to the bedroom, and put a pillow over Teddy's eyes, and took her second camera.

"What are you doing?" Teddy said.

"Be quiet, young man or I will punish you more severely."

"Oh please, don't."

Sally returned to the kitchen. She took the bags out of the freezer, and neatly lined them up on the counter, with the heads facing her. She took several photos of the bags. She looked at the photos. Then she opened each bag to expose the birds' heads. The birds partially stuck to the insides of the bags. While trying to get a bird out, she put a one inch tear in the one of the bags. "Shoot."

The heads of two birds poked out of the bags completely. Half of the head of a third bird stuck out of the bag. She took some more pictures.

She spotted the copy of Teddy's Brown diploma hanging by a magnet. She removed it, place it between the birds, and took more pictures. After returning the diploma to the door, and the birds to the freezer, she got another Coke, and returned to Teddy's room.

She put the phone back in place, and hit the record button. Then she removed the pillow from Teddy's face.

"Where have you been?" he said.

She gently placed the Coke can on his forehead, and then removed it.

"Oh that feels good. Please can I have some?"

She placed the can a few inches from his face, and pulled the tab. "Swoosh."

He said, "Mmmmmmm."

She moved the can six inches above his open mouth, and poured some out. The Coke landed near his mouth, on his cheek, and then it flowed down onto his neck.

"Taste good, Teddy?"

"Yes."

She gently slapped him. "What?"

"Yes, Mistress Sally, the Coke tastes good."

"That's better, Teddy."

She then gently moved a riding crop up and down his belly. She moved her face within a foot of his, looked him in the eyes, and smiled. "I think a little starting and stopping, a little frustration, … that's kind of fun, don't you think?"

"Yes, yes it is Mistress Sally."

"That's good. Now I think you've been a bad boy, don't you? …."

* * *

* * *

It was 1:00 in the morning. Teddy had finished. He was exhausted, happy and ready for sleep. Sally put her clothes on, and placed the second cell phone in her purse. She untied Teddy. He slowly got out of bed, put on his underwear, and walked over to the first cell phone on the bureau. He picked it up and looked at the screen. "You weren't using this as an alarm. What were you going to do with the video?"

"It was going to be a gift to you. A way to remember a wonderful evening of bliss."

"Yea. Right." He deleted the video, and went to the trash bin on the phone, and deleted it from there as well.

"You knew I was filming you. You liked the idea of me filming you, didn't you? The adrenaline rush of possibly being blackmailed? That excited you."

Teddy did not respond.

"I have your number," Sally said. "I'll call you."

She walked out of the room quickly. Teddy was moving slowly. As she opened the front door to the house he said, "I'd invite you to stay, but we both have to get some sleep before work …."

He heard the door close, and then her car pull out of the driveway.

The Blackmail

Emily was at work. She called Teddy. "How'd you like the video I sent you?"

"Who is this? Sally?"

"Men have strange tastes, but your tastes are really twisted."

"Who is this? Why are you calling?"

"You owe me something."

Teddy stared at the mermaid figurehead hanging from his wall. "Sally, you bitch."

"I'm not Sally. We need to set up a time to talk. We'll need fifteen minutes to half an hour. Is now good?"

"No. How about 2:00 today? Where do you want to meet?"

"I'll call you at 2:00." She hung up.

* * *

At 2:05 Emily called Teddy on a disposable cell phone. "Hi Teddy. It's me."

"Who is this?"

"You've caused me a lot of problems."

"What are you talking about?"

"Serious problems."

"Do you want money?"

"No. You've done something that you need to undo. That's all."

"What did I do? Do you need an abortion?"

"That's disgusting."

"So … what are you talking about?"

"You were on Fox News on TV talking about gopher turtles."

"If you're from PETA, I didn't hurt those turtles."

Emily was looking out her office window. She watched some sparrows in the distance eating from a bird feeder outside a condo. "I'm not from PETA. A friend of mine owns the land that you were trespassing on where you supposedly found those turtles."

"Lots of people go on that land. So what if I was trespassing? No one ever gets arrested for that. I didn't do any damage."

"You did plenty of damage to my friend. You see, because of the turtles my friend can't sell the land."

Teddy played with a pen on his desk. "I'm sorry for your friend, but that's the turtles' fault, not mine."

"Not really. Those turtles, gopher turtles, don't live around here."

"With global warming and all, they probably moved down here. Animals move around you know."

"That makes no sense. If global warming was causing them to move, they'd move to a cooler place, not a warmer place. They'd move north not south. Are you an idiot? I know you planted the turtles on the property."

"I didn't plant those turtles. I was looking for Yuma birds, and I stumbled upon the turtles."

"Why were you looking for Yuma?"

"None of your F'n business. Lots of people look for Yuma's after they hit the news."

"You planted the Yuma too, didn't you?"

"You're delusional."

"Why did you plant the gopher turtles?"

"Are you deaf or stupid? I just said I didn't plant them."

Emily was watching the video that Sally had taken of Teddy. "Let's change the subject. I'm watching the video of you tied to the bed in your underwear. I'm glad you had such a good time."

"So what?"

"As you know, my friend has a buyer for the land. The turtles are blocking the sale. You need to publicly admit that you planted the turtles and also admit it to the state EPA."

"You're crazy. I'm not going to do that. That would ruin my career. Plus, I didn't do it."

"I would think planting endangered species on someone's property would help you in your environmental career. The sleazier you are, the more the radical Greenies like you. Who cares if you destroy someone's life. It's a sacrifice for the cause."

"I wouldn't do stuff like that."

"President Obama had no qualms destroying coal miner's lives in West Virgina when he shut the coal mines down."

"What are you, a right-wing nut job? Do you have a gun trained on my head?"

"Admit to planting the turtles, or I send the video to your bosses and then put it on Facebook and tell the world on Twitter."

"I don't care that much about the video. It is embarrassing, but it has nothing to do with my job. Every day you see in the news public figures doing all sorts of embarrassing things, and they are only hurt for just a short time. Then they bounce back pretty quickly. Congressman Glickman from New Jersey was texting pictures of his wiener to some teenage girl, for lord's sake."

"YouTube as well Teddy."

"Go ahead. I didn't plant the turtles. If I figure out who you are, I'm going to get you arrested for blackmail." He hung up.

Emily stared out the window for a few minutes, then called Sally. "That pig didn't care about the video. He wouldn't admit that he planted the turtles. Crap. Crap. Crap." She could feel her head beginning to spin with anger. She was about to lose control.

"You've got to be kidding. The stuff on that video grosses me out, and that says a lot. Boy, he must work for and hang out with some strange folks if he doesn't care if they see that."

Emily was hyperventilating into the phone. "I'm going to get that mother-f'er if it's the last thing I do. I know he planted those turtles. Lisa's photo shows the turtle in his car."

"Who is Lisa? What photo?"

Emily told Sally about Lisa and the photo of Teddy and the turtle in his car.

"I didn't know you were that certain he had planted the turtles. Why not just get Lisa to say she saw him drive up with the turtles?"

"She's just a kid. People would believe her. They'd believe Teddy. Plus, he might be a little crazy, and I don't want him to hurt her. If I could just come up with something else on Teddy, and combine it with Lisa's photo, that might put him over the edge."

"OK. I have an idea for attacking this from a different angle."

Sally and Emily discussed the new strategy. "It might work, but there are a lot of moving parts," Emily said. "A lot of places where things could go wrong."

"When can you pay me my $3,000? I got you the video."

"No way Sally. I only owe it if the land sells. I would have preferred the lower fee, and pay you up front. No way."

"OK. OK. I'm just getting a little worried this won't work."

"A deal's a deal. Plus, I already paid you $500 toward your fee. I won't get that back. I got nothing for my $500."

"You got a beautiful video. A work of art. Submit it to the Sundance Film Festival. Maybe someone will buy it."

"Sorry. Not enough good dialog."

"Well. Good luck with Teddy. Call me if you need my expertise again."

* * *

* * *

Jerry was in his car driving to one of Mermaid Inc's biggest clients, The Happy Clam Marina and Store in Fort Lauderdale. He had just been reviewing the financial records of Mermaid Inc. They were still losing money, a little higher amount each month. He was having sleep problems. He had friends who had gone to great colleges who were working as nannies at wages slightly higher than the minimum wage. And the hours were horrible, and some of them were treated like indentured servants. *Maybe I shouldn't have gone to college. But the connections I made were good. I met Emily, and got this job from her. Doesn't pay well, but it's really interesting, and I get to make a lot of my own decisions. Great experience. Looks good on my resume.*

He parked his car at The Happy Clam Marina parking lot, walked into the store, and told the clerk he had an appointment with Tom, the store manager. The marina store was large, and sold practically any item that a boater could want.

"Good to see you Jerry. So you said on the phone you want to talk about your mermaid cleats."

"Yes. Sales have dipped and we're trying to figure out why."

"I love the cleats. Both the smaller decorative ones, and the larger ones for the docks. I can't take anymore into inventory now though. We are sitting on a good number."

"Do you have any idea why sales have slowed?" Jerry said.

"I'm not really sure. My sales for all the products in the store have been steady. We haven't seen a dip in overall sales. I had a few customers who were using your mermaid cleats come in and buy regular cleats. They said that their boats almost came loose from the dock because the lines had frayed, and they thought the problem might be caused be the mermaid cleats. They weren't sure, because other things can fray a line. You know — a line rubbing against the sharp corner of even a wooden dock can fray a line. But they said their main fraying problems were with lines tied to your mermaid cleats."

"That's surprising. You'd think a cleat's a cleat."

"Yes. You'd think so."

The two men talked some more about the marine store and marina businesses, and then Jerry walked down to The Happy Clam docks. The wind was blowing hard and there was a heavy chop in the water. The boats tied to the dock were moving strongly with the chop and the wind. Jerry was happy to see that about half the boats were using his mermaid cleats. Boat owners had told him they liked the atmosphere that the cleats helped create at the marina. There were metal flamingos on the docks along with some small palm trees, plastic sea turtles, nautically decorated 'Welcome' and 'All Aboard' signs, and other sea and beach decorations. Jerry had been to the docks on the weekends, and had seen that many of the boat owners liked to just relax on their boats at the docks, treating them like a floating weekend cottage.

He stopped at one of the boats that was tied to the dock with mermaid cleats. He stared at a cleat as the rope strained and slackened with the rocking of the boat and with the wind and the waves. The mermaid had a devilish smile and her eyes followed Teddy's as he looked at her. She had large, firm breasts that were covered with sea shells. Like most men, Jerry loved womens' breasts. He was fascinated by them. However, he loved small ones, not large. His first three girlfriends all had small breasts, and from the many happy hours he had spent kissing them, he had developed a strong obsession with small breasts.

He had made the original design for the mermaid cleats, and had given the mermaid small breasts. He and Emily had then sent his design to an artist for a more polished rendering. She had immigrated from Venezuela, and insisted that everyone, men and women, liked large breasts. Implants were a huge business in Venezuela. Jerry and Emily had argued with her and she had reluctantly agreed to make them smaller, but they were still large. The design went to the forge to make the mold for the cleats, and after that it was too expensive to change the mold. Sales had started strong, and the controversy over the big breasts had died.

The dock rocked with the waves. Jerry was staring at the breasts, and the rope crossing the breasts, moving rhythmically with the waves, when he saw a small strand of the rope break. It broke at the spot where it was rubbing against the edge of the mermaid's breast. He went down the dock and looked at a bunch of different mermaid cleats. The rope on each cleat was fraying in the exact same spot, where it rubbed against the mermaid's breast. The fraying wasn't severe, but it was obvious when he looked closely. All the ropes would eventually break over time.

He called Emily and told her what he had found.

"I'm going to drive down tomorrow, and take a look for myself," she said.

"Yes. You should."

* * *

Emily texted to Teddy the picture of Teddy standing next to his car with his hands down his pants. The text said, "You shouldn't do this in front of young girls. The bubbas in prison don't take kindly to your type."

"Leave me alone or I'll call the police," he texted back.

"The police will love that photo."

Emily got no answer back.

"If you like playing with your dinky out in public where kids get their school bus, that's your business," Emily texted. "What I find interesting is that gopher turtle sitting in your car in the picture."

No answer.

She texted, “A person can get into a lot of legal trouble transporting threatened species.”

No answer.

She texted, “Drip. Drip. Drip. It’s beginning to accumulate. A picture of you transporting a threatened species. A weird S&M video. A picture with your hands down your pants, sweat dripping down your face. A silly grin.”

He texted, “I didn’t put the turtles on the land.”

“I’m not going to ask you to admit that or anything else. I want something different from you this time. Easier. ”

“OK. Lets talk in half an hour.”

Half an hour later Emily called Teddy. “I think your career is toast if those photos of the turtles in your car get out.”

“Hey, you told me that your were going to back off. Do you want to talk or not?”

“Yes, here is the new proposal for you so that you can save your butt. I want you to … .”

“I was saving that turtle. It was hurt. I didn’t bring it with me. I was taking it. And I didn’t know it was a gopher turtle. Uh, er. I think it wasn’t a gopher turtle.”

“Let’s stay on topic, enviro man. This is what you will do for me. You will … .”

“No. I want to talk about the photo. That’s bull shit.”

“OK. If you want, ass-hole. It is a gopher turtle. Easy to prove. Ignorance of the environmental regulations is no excuse. An 11 year old girl was arrested because she pulled an endangered woodpecker out of her cat’s mouth. Then she went to Home Depot to get a box for the bird. A Fish and Wildlife person happened to be shopping there, saw the bird, and had the girl arrested. Google it. You have some real wackos in the environmental business, and you’re one of them.
The government enviro people are just as bad.”

“I’m not worried. Saving an injured turtle will only make me look good. I’m probably even licensed to save an injured animal.”

“BS. Probably not. It doesn’t matter. You were planting it on the land. You weren’t saving it.”

“That’s ridiculous. Why would I put turtles on someone’s land?”

“Because you’re a wacko. Just look at the S&M video of you.”

“*Fifty Shades of Gray* was a big hit with you suburban women. The book and the movie. People don’t care. I’d probably get dates if people saw that video.”

“No, in *Fifty Shades,* the woman was tied up, not the man.”

“I don’t care about the video of me. Release it if you want.”

"I have proof that you brought the turtle with you in the car. The Fish and Wildlife people will be all over you."

"There is no proof."

"Do you really want to take that chance? Maybe your neighbor saw you put the turtles in your car. I know where you live. The S&M video was taken at your house. A bird watcher told me he saw you bring the turtles to the land. The birders hang out in the bushes looking for Yumas. They're friends of mine. You probably planted the Yuma too."

"So you're playing Russian roulette with me?"

"No. The gun's only pointed at your head, not mine. Bad analogy Mr. Brown University boy. But let's get back to why we're having this conversation. I have a new deal for you. You don't get hurt in any way."

"What is it?"

"You will get someone else to plant some gopher turtles on the land. We'll film them doing it, and go to the EPA or Fish and Wildlife with the film."

"That's quite a plan."

"You'll be screwed if you don't do what I say."

"So I won't be connected at all to the turtles? I don't need to be at the land when the turtles are released? What I have to do is convince someone else to release the turtles?"

"Yes. That's all correct."

"It sounds OK on the surface, but I don't see how I could convince anyone to release endangered turtles onto the land."

"You had a motive to plant the turtles. Someone else could have the same motive."

"My ... no, I didn't, I didn't plant any turtles."

"OK. Yea. We've already been down that road. You didn't plant any turtles. But let's talk theoretically. If we can dream up a reason why someone would want to plant an endangered species on someone else's land, then maybe you could lead someone else into doing it as well."

Teddy was staring at the mermaid statue in his office. "I want to finish this conversation in person. I think that would be more appropriate, and safer, for both of us."

"You're probably right. How about The Waterstone in an hour?"

"See you there."

*   *   *

Emily walked into the outdoor restaurant at The Waterstone Resort and Marina, saw Teddy at the quiet bar, and walked up to him. It was 2:00 in the afternoon. "You look different with your clothes on," she said.

"Not as good, I'm sure. And you look like a freshman in college."

"Thanks. Let's move to that table by the water. We'll have lots of privacy."

The bar and the dining area sat on a stone patio directly on The Intercoastal Waterway. The current was running quickly five feet below the patio, and the fish were competing for scraps of food that some of the customers had thrown into the water. Over-looking the patio was a short draw bridge with a grated road in the middle that caused the car tires to give off a choppy sound. Across the waterway was a twenty story pink resort. The sun was shining, there was a slight breeze, and the temperature was perfect.

They sat down and Emily ordered a Coke.

"So this is your line of work, being an environmentalist and all. Any ideas?"

"You've got me."

Emily stared into his eyes with an expressionless face. He smiled slightly, lips closed, and turned to look at the water. Emily waited a few moments, and then said, "Oh, I bet you could use your imagination and make a guess. I read about a fanatical environmental professor who was planting some type of grouse on a farmer's land. The government would have blocked the farmer from using his land if there was grouse there. The guy would have lost his livelihood. The environmentalist didn't care at all about the guy. I don't think the news article ever said what the motive was. Nuts do these things."

"Interesting story."

"A motive might be that they wanted to prevent development. But why? Or they might want the publicity from discovering the animals. Why would someone want publicity? Because they like publicity? Does it get them anything? Or the motive might be hatred of land developers. Or hatred of capitalism. Creating a new habitat? Or love of animals. But the environmentalist who planted that grouse, killed the grouse first. So it wouldn't fly away, I guess. Maybe he thought - sacrifice one grouse to help other grouses with more habitat. Eagles get killed as a sacrifice for wind energy. Anyway, I'm just trying to get your brain in gear."

"I'm drawing a blank. It's going to be hard to find someone."

"Really. You're in the enviro business. I bet you can dream up something that I couldn't think of."

"You know you just sprung this on me an hour ago. You've had some time to think about this."

"Maybe you're not very creative."

"I need some time."

"I don't have much time," Emily said.

"Why not?"

"None of your business."

They stared at the boats going by for a few minutes.

Emily said, "You don't have any ideas. So here is the plan unless you come up with something better." Emily explained the strategy to Teddy.

Teddy thought for a few minutes, and said, “It’s sleazy but it might work. I just need to be careful so that nothing is linked to me . OK, I’ll take the first few steps, and we’ll see how it goes.”

“It will work.”

“So once the plan is done, and you, or whoever, is able to sell the land, you will destroy the video and the photo. You’ll have copies. What about the copies? Where is my protection?”

“Yea, right. You’ll want more than ‘you’ll have to trust us.’”

“I don’t trust you.”

“Hire a lawyer, and put a copy of the video and the photo in the lawyer’s file. Include a statement that the material was used to get concessions from you. The statement should be notarized so you can prove when the file was put together. Proving it was put together before you had any need for it. If I later release either the video or the photo, then the lawyer’s file can be used to come after me for getting concessions from you.”

“You mean for blackmailing me.”

“Concessions.”

“That gives me some protection but not 100 percent.”

“You don’t have any other option. You know … I’m not asking for very much from you. If I was untrustworthy, I’d also be asking you for a lot of money in addition to clearing the turtle problem.”

“Maybe.”

“Well, you have to trust me somewhat. Otherwise if we don’t have a deal, I’ll release the video and the photo.”

“I’ll do it.” He got up and walked out.

* * *

Emily was sitting on the balcony at her apartment in the early evening. She had been to the marina and had seen that her cleats were causing the boat ropes to chafe. Breast reduction would be a life-saver for Mermaid Inc.

Jerry had made a copy of the original rendering, and using colored pencils had reduced the mermaid’s breasts. He had sent the picture to the forge company to get a quote for a new mold for smaller breasted cleats.

Jerry called Emily. “A new mold will cost $350.”

“Ouch. These expenses are killing me. My bank account is being bled dry. I know we have to do it. Is there any way you can throw in some money Jerry? Maybe ask Brittany if she can help. After all, your jobs depend on it.”

“I can put up $100, and I’ll ask Brittany what she can do.”

“Great. Thanks. Get the new mold done and I’m sure they’ll give us thirty days to pay.”

“No problem. Our credit is good with them, and we’re a small account. I’ll order the mold, and also order 100 new cleats with the new design."

"Make it 150. Also come up with a new marketing plan so customers know we have a new and improved cleat. Change the colors on the mermaid too so people can easily see that we have a new design. Not everyone ogles at big boobs like you do."

"I like small boobs. I've told you that before."

"Yea, right."

"I do," Jerry said. "Do you want to see the new colors before I order?"

"No. Just text me a picture when you make the order, or before, if you can remember."

"What do you think about replacing all the old cleats with new ones? Giving existing customers free cleats? It would be good customer service, and also good marketing. We could do it on the weekends when there are lots of people at their boats. We could play music while we replace the cleats, and wear t-shirts with the company name on them. We could sell cleats to new customers while we service the existing customers."

"Hey - Brittany and I can dress up like mermaids."

"Yea. Yea. Great idea. The middle-aged men will be all over the two of you. You'll sell them lots of cleats. You'll have them eating out of your hands."

"Ha. I know they will. And I know where to rent the costumes."

"This is sounding good. We'll need to give The Happy Clam marina store a cut of the new sales. They sell the cleats in their store, so they will lose sales."

"Or maybe they'll gain sales if our marketing works. Why don't you bargain with the manager and see what you can do. You're right — I don't want to go behind their backs and sell cleats on their docks without his permission. If this works, we can try this at our other marina customers."

"Great. We have a plan. Better than just wallowing around. Talk to you later."

* * *

Jerry received a shipment of the new small-breasted mermaid cleats, and then Jerry, Emily and Brittany went to The Happy Clam Marina on a sunny Saturday morning. Emily and Brittany put on mermaid costumes. They walked down the docks handing out the new cleats free of charge to the people who already owned the old cleats. Jerry wore a bright blue t-shirt that said 'Mermaid Cleat.com — Where All Your Cleat Dreams Can Come True.'

The marina manager had agreed to have his crew install the new cleats free of charge since the new cleats would be safer. There had been a lot of talk among the boaters about possible problems with the old cleats. The boaters felt safer with the new cleats, and sales increased quickly. The boaters, especially the men and lesbians, had carefully studied the large breasts and had seen the chafing. The men kept the discarded cleats hidden in their closets at home. The lesbians proudly displayed them on their coffee tables.

The following day was a clear, beautiful Sunday, and Jerry and Brittany went to two other large marina clients, and did the same routine that they had done at The Happy Clam. Those customers were also happy with the new cleats, and sales increased steadily. Jerry ordered more cleats from the forge company, with payment due in 30 days. Jerry and Brittany waited until the following weekend before servicing their other marina customers. Walking up and down the docks, Brittany dressed as a mermaid, Jerry in the t-shirt, they talked to customers and sold cleats.

Jerry also made changes to their website, Facebook site and other internet sites to let customers know that the cleats had been re-designed. Sales grew immediately, and Mermaid Inc quickly started earning a small but steady and solid profit, after all wages had been paid. Jerry knew that other people had grown rich in the past from selling Beanie Babies, Pet Rocks, Poke-mon, raccoon hats in the 1850's and other far-fetched ideas. Why not mermaid cleats? Not just for boats, but for window blinds, coffee tables, gay bars and male fantasies. The sky was the limit.

Let's Try That Again

Marsha was the local manager Earth Zealots, another environmental non-profit located in Boca Raton. As they say, 'Why do you rob banks?' 'Because that's where the money is.' Earth Zealots was organized like The Environmental Hounds, with a central national office, regional offices and local offices. They liked Boca because they could mine the rich people for tax deductible donations. The rich environmentalists, like Leonardo Dicaprio and John Kerry, liked giving money because the money off-set the huge amounts of carbon dioxide that their many mansions, jets and yachts discharged into the atmosphere. Plus the donations off-set, in some way or other, the thousands of eagles and other raptors that the wind farms, the darlings of the environmentalists, killed each year. It was like a self-sustaining biological paradise, or so they thought. Life was good. They were in-tune with the world.

Many of the extremely rich liberals considered themselves to be environmentalists because this made them feel like they were giving back. After they wrote their donation checks, they did not really track how the money was spent. They did not realize that their children often could not find good jobs after graduating from college, because environmental regulations had destroyed many of the jobs in the United States. Then their children would get menial jobs at the environmental agencies. These jobs had little responsibility, challenge, or even meaning, and paid little. Their children would then ask why they had studied so hard in prep school and college if all that awaited them upon graduation were lousy jobs. Of course, some got good jobs. It was not all bleak. Especially if you had connections, like the Clintons, Bush's and Obamas.

Marsha, however was the manager, the head-honcho, and she had a rewarding job. *Thank God* her parents had said when she got the job. Despite her being homely with a small black mustache and medium sized, sagging tits, with small black hairs growing out of her nipples, Teddy had done her anyway. It was some of the best sex he had ever had, and that was saying a lot. He had met her at the reception welcoming her to the area, thrown by the local business and non-profit community.

She was 28 and had gone to Brimheid University in Massachusetts. She was dedicated to her job, and to environmentalism. In college she had started a group that stopped a textile factory in Lawrence, Massachusetts from dumping arsenic in the Lawrence River. Her group protested outside the expensive homes of the factory executives, and blocked the executives from driving their cars out of their driveways in Wellesley. Reported death threats against the executives' were never substantiated. The factories shut down as they could not afford to correctly dispose of the arsenic. The workers had to sell their homes, and move to other states, out of New England, where factory jobs still existed.

Her romantic life had always been a little spotty and it had not gotten any better after she had moved to Boca Raton. Her fling with Teddy had been her brightest moment.

Unlike most of Teddy's conquests, Marsha was someone he had stayed in touch with, but on a professional rather than a romantic basis. He had not liked her little peach fuzz tickling his upper lip, nor did he like staring at it while eating dinner. He did find the nipple hair to be erotic. With Marsha he lived by the adage, 'Keep your friends close and your enemies even closer.'

He liked Marsha. She was smart and aggressive. She had been a wildcat in bed. Earth Zealots however was the enemy. The Zealots were worse than factories that dumped pollution into the rivers. Earth Zealots competed with Environmental Hounds for donations from rich liberals. One of Teddy's main job responsibilities was to squeeze money out of these people. Spotting a sucker with rich, liberal guilt was like mining a wide, deep vein of gold. If you mined it correctly, it could bring untold riches for many, many years. It was a symbiotic relationship as the rich liberal received great benefits — he or she enjoyed their trips to Europe, cruises to the Antarctic, mansions and yachts much more because of their donations. These goodies were now enjoyed guilt free.

Teddy had called Marsha to meet for lunch. They met at JB's on the Beach in Deerfield Beach. They had a table at the edge of the patio next to the beach under an umbrella. The sun came in and out from behind the large puffy clouds.

"So it was nice of you to call me Teddy. It's good to see you."

"Glad you had the time. It's good to see you too. So what's new with you? How are things at Earth Zealots?"

She laughed. "Why? Are you looking for a job? You really enjoy being underneath me."

He laughed. "Yea. I do. Or did."

"We could make it a 'do' if you want." She smiled at him and moved her eye brows up and down.

They small-talked for ten minutes before Teddy said, "After that TV news report about us finding the threatened turtles, our funding has gone way up. It was really satisfying saving those turtles."

"I bet it was. What's going on with that?"

"Fish and Wildlife are doing a study to confirm that the turtles are nesting on the land. But any land development is temporarily blocked while the study is going on. It should be quick. But it's the government, so you know, quick for them can be forever. That's good."

Marsha took a bite of bread, and a small piece stuck to her tooth, below her mustache. "Yea, the feds took seven years to study the Keystone XL Pipeline from Canada, almost the entire administration of President Obama. President Obama did a great job."

"Yea, and he sold it well to the idiots."

The waitress gave them their waters, and they looked at the menus.

"I thought your donations would go up after that TV spot. I'm jealous. Ours have gone down, pretty much right after you were on TV."

"We got so much extra cash, we're just banking it. Maybe you'll end up working for me. I'll let you be on top sometimes though."

She giggled. "Good. I like being on top."

Teddy could see her nipples harden. "I'll say. You practically woke up the neighborhood with your moaning the last time you were on top." He laughed.

They looked at the menus some more, and then ordered.

"Our donations across the country are not doing that well," she said. "We've had a few higher-ups jump ship to other non-profits, including yours."

Teddy had read about both of those things in *Environmentalist Today,* the environmentalist trade magazine, where you could also buy solar panel installation franchises, camouflage gear, night-vision goggles, hire professional protesters for an hourly fee, and trade environmental tax credits. The latest edition had the actress Dana Hemdrip bent forward, with a baby penguin looking out from between her massive cleavage, with a starry eyed look in her eyes. The lead article was *Don't Be Fooled - There Is No Upside to Global Warming.*

You could also buy a swimsuit issue featuring two over-weight, pasty-skinned 65 year-old men wearing Speedos, clearly showing their junk. One was an ex-politician turned film-maker. The other a leftest documentary film-maker. Both were very rich. Both were climate-change religious fanatics. They had previously been global-warming religious fanatics, but had found it difficult to convince the average person that the world was in fact warming, when the average person noted from their own observations that the world did not seem to be warming much at all. Obviously the average person was not as intelligent as these two elites. The two were very disappointed when major hurricanes did not cause massive death and destruction on the East Coast in the last fifteen years, as the global-warming scientists had assured everybody would happen. The men could not say, 'I told you so … you deplorables.'

In the magazine the two men stood in various poses at a swanky beach resort, as titillating as any *Sports Illustrated* swim-suit spread. Well, not quite. All proceeds from sales of the issue went to the 'Environmental Attack and Destroy Group' whose motto was 'Live Like A Caveman, Keep the Environment Carbon Free.' In the last photo one of the gentlemen was rubbing pools of organic, GMO-free aloe lotion over the other's hairy chest. You could not see the fronts of their Speedos in the photo, luckily. The issue did not sell well.

Teddy said, "People leaving your agency might be good for you. More opportunity for you to move up. That's if your funding doesn't get really bad. I have the opposite problem. There aren't many openings to move up to. And now it could get worse, if some of your people move into those spots above me."

They drank their drinks and watched the people in the restaurant.

"It's too bad we can't somehow combine our advantages to benefit both of us," Teddy said.

"What do you mean?"

"At my place we have lots of money, but no higher level jobs to move up into. At your place you don't have much money, but you have good jobs to move into. I feel caged in where I am."

"Oh, poor Teddy, with those views of the Intercoastal."

"Views aren't everything." He was staring at her nipples. She pushed her chest out slightly.

"I'm surprised you want to move up. You seem to have a good gig here. You do hands-on work on actual environmental issues. At a higher level you'd do less hands-on work, and more organizing and managing people."

"And more money. I like doing organizing work. And money."

"Yea, some of those higher-ups make tons of money. Over $400,000 per year I bet. Those rich hedge fund people and CEO's can really dump some big donations."

Teddy watched the young waitress bend over to pick up a napkin. "It's a good gig, if you can get up that high up."

"If our funding went up, would you consider jumping ship over to Earth Zealots?"

"I'd certainly think about it. We just happened to get lucky finding those gopher turtles and getting the publicity."

"Really? Lucky? Somehow Teddy I don't … ."

"Maybe you'll have similar luck. Although truthfully, the chances are like playing the lottery — just stumbling upon some endangered species, well it really doesn't happen, not that often."

She stared at him. "Yea, really almost never. When I saw you on TV I thought 'this is like winning at Atlantic City. What are the odds that Teddy would find endangered species? Really low.'"

Teddy smiled and took a bite. "Maybe you can make your own luck."

She stared at him. "I had wondered, was it more than luck?"

"Ha, ha. Yes, it was Divine Intervention."

She watched a boat going by. "I believe people can make their own luck sometimes. In college I made a little of my own luck by pouring a little cyanide in a river. The cyanide helped shut a factory down that was doing bad things to the river. The protests I had organized against the factory, well, that was how I made a name for myself in this field. It got me launched and one thing lead to another, and then to this job."

"I remember at your welcoming reception here in Boca they talked about your experiences from college. You had organized protests against some factory somewhere in Massachusetts."

"That was it. So I made my own luck in college, maybe I'll make my own luck now."

Teddy said, "Just be careful."

"Maybe if I try enough I can find some gopher turtles or some other endangered species on some land somewhere."

They watched a jet ski jumping the waves in the Atlantic. The clouds had gone and the sun was bright.

"A friend of mine said he just bought an exotic animal for a pet from a guy in Orlando. I can get the name and number of the guy if you want it. The guy sells other exotic animals."

"Oooohhh. I like your way of thinking. Yea - call me with the guy's cell."

"I'll have it tonight."

"You'll get the best bang for your buck if you happen to find an endangered species on the same land that I found the turtles on."

"Why's that?"

"The land has gotten a lot of publicity because of a pending sale to a company that has been in the news a lot. You might get no publicity if you find an animal on land in the middle of nowhere."

"Mmmm. Kind of makes a little sense. My adrenaline is beginning to run, and it feels good. I think I've been a little too stagnant in my job. This will be good."

They small talked some more, finished their lunches and paid the bill. In the parking lot Teddy said, "I'll call you with that guy's number."

"This was a fun nooner. We should do a real nooner some day."

"I'd like that."

"We should go out some night."

"OK. Let's text each other. Bye, bye." *I hope I don't have to hop in the sack with her. Although she likes being on top....*

* * *

After talking to Teddy, Marsha felt more energized than she had in a year. This would be exciting, and would bring back some of the mystique and allure she held felt running the environmental club in college. Plus Earth Zealots needed cash, and the publicity would be great

She began researching what animal species she could use. It needed to be rare, but not too rare for it to be believable. An arctic fox in Florida? No, that wouldn't do. A bird would be great because people loved birds. But birds fly away. She could not identify a good flightless bird as there were none that might live naturally in Florida. Ostriches and Emus, no they wouldn't work.

There were several snakes listed as endangered or threatened, but if she planted some snakes, they would be difficult for someone to find. She did not like handling snakes except for Teddy's snake and ones like it. She especially was afraid of poisonous snakes. Constrictors she could live with. Salamanders, frogs and skinks were a little easier to find than snakes would be, but they were all small, and hard to find.

She read about the alligator snapping turtle. It was somewhat common further north, but would be very rare in South Florida, though not unheard of. They lived in northern Florida and in several states north of Florida. Some had been found outside their normal range. One had been found in St. Louis and another in Washington, DC, although that one had probably been someone's pet. Alligator snapping turtles were not classified as endangered or threatened though. They were classified as SSC which stood for a 'state species of special concern.' Not as serious as 'threatened.' Marsha wanted 'threatened' or 'endangered' to get the most publicity.

She had followed what Florida Fish and Wildlife was doing in their investigation of the gopher turtles on Emily's land. Fish and Wildlife were unsure if the turtles had been naturally living there. So they were investigating the habitat for vegetation, water sources, burrow size and age, and the distance and location of other gopher turtles. If she was able to find more gopher turtles on the land, she would be able to get great publicity. Her find would help substantiate for Fish and Wildlife that the turtles were living there naturally, and it would be a great follow-up story for TV news.

Her protesters would be at the site as soon as her turtles were discovered. They had once picketed at a the home of a man who had cut off the head of a Burmese python. The snake had wrapped itself around a Florida sandhill crane. The snake was not natural to Florida. The bird was. The protesters did such a good job harassing the man, and threatening his life, and the lives of his wife and children, that the family had to move, sell their house at a loss and change their last name.

Marsha was able to buy gopher turtles from Teddy's seller in Orlando.

She and Teddy had had several dates after they had met for lunch. Whenever she made any hints that she was up to something, Teddy would change the subject. The secrecy made it even more exciting for Marsha. This was better than shoplifting. She could feel her heart beating faster as she planned her attack. She felt good. She felt excited again like she had in college. She felt alive.

The day she had bought the turtles, Teddy stopped by her apartment. The three turtles were sitting in a box in her kitchen. Teddy looked into the box. "Those are cute."

He stuck his hand into the box, and wriggled his fingers about 6 inches in front of one of one of the turtles. "I'm pretty fast, you know, Marsha."

"Not for me. You're just about the right speed. Not too quick. Hmm, hmm."

Teddy grinned. "He looks like he's sleeping. I've been bitten by a turtle before, and it really hurt."

"Is that where you got that V-shaped mark near your willie?"

"Yes, nasty little guy."

"I'll have to give it the Marsha special treatment next time I'm down there."

"Hmm, baby, hmmmm. Keep it coming."

"You're a wild man Teddy. 'Me Tarzan. You Jane.' What kind of turtle bit you?"

"I don't know. I never found out."

He removed his hand from the box. "I guess they're not in the mood to play. They should make fun pets for you Marsha."

"Yes. They're so cuddly and cute. I like to curl up to them on my couch while I watch old episodes of *Friends."*

"Sounds cozy and warm. I bet they'll be expensive and difficult to feed."

"Probably cheap. I think they'll eat iceberg lettuce and regular vegetables. I'm worried that I'll kill them if I keep them too long."

"Yea, I almost killed a boa once by mistake because I couldn't get it to eat the mice I was feeding it. I gave it dead mice that had been frozen. I boiled the mice first before I gave them to the snake. That didn't work. So I tried live mice. The snake just sat there and stared. One mouse climbed up on top of the snake's head, and eventually started gnawing on the snake. I got the mouse out of the cage. The snake didn't eat for weeks. Its cage got gross."

"So what did you do?"

"I threw it into my backyard. Those things move fast. Amazingly healthy even after my care."

"Teddy, you're not supposed to throw boas out into the wild. You know that."

"I know. But I needed to do something with it, and if I kept it in the cage, I thought it would die. About a year later the cats in the neighborhood started disappearing, but I don't think my boa could have grown fast enough to eat cats."

"Probably not. You should have cut it's head off. That would have been more humane."

"Yes, like when they killed Michael Vick's dogs when they learned the dogs had been bred for fighting. That was the best thing for their welfare."

"Or in San Francisco — it's illegal to sell live dogs, but it's ok to sell dead ones to eat."

They both giggled, and looked at the turtles.

Marsha said, "I hope to get rid of them soon."

"Get rid of what?"

"The turtles."

"That sounds smart. How soon?"

"Tomorrow."

"You're working tomorrow, aren't you."

"Yes. I hope to get rid of them first thing in the morning, before work."

Teddy looked at the turtles. "Did you see that some California billionaire gave a million dollars to some environmental non-profit in D.C.?"

"Yea. Those lucky bastards."

"Do you want to order take-out? It's on me."

"Sure. What are you in the mood for?"

* * *

It was early morning and Emily was standing behind a bush about 50 yards from the street a short distance off the main trail on her property. The bush was on the edge of a small clearing, close to where Teddy had planted the turtles.

The sun was bright to the east, but the thick palm and pine tree cover created an undulating blanket of shadow and sharp light moving over the underbrush below. It was a cool 65 degrees. The forest was quiet. There was a musky smell.

Emily was wearing a camouflage shirt, pants and baseball hat, and a camera with a telescopic lens hung from a strap around her neck. She wore a small back-pack. Showing through its mesh was a small bird book.

Brittany was hiding nearby. She was dressed the same as Emily, and also had a bird identification book. She had sewn a 'Southern Florida Birding Society' patch onto her baseball hat.

Emily's phone vibrated. "A car has just parked on the street next to the trail opening." It was Ricardo. "It looks like Marsha's car. A woman is getting out. She has a small black mustache and medium-size saggy tits. It's Marsha. She's standing by the back of her car, looking around, drinking from a cup."

"OK."

"She's just standing there. I'll tell you when she moves."

Ricardo was parked far up the street from the trail opening. He was sitting in his car looking at Marsha through a large telephoto lens on his camera. His car had tinted windows. Ricardo had seen pictures of Marsha on Earth Zealot's website.

Ricardo said, "She has opened the trunk and has pulled out a box about a foot long. All I'm able to get in my camera is Marsha and a box. Not turtles."

"Keep watching."

"OK, I'll get pictures later."

A few minutes passed and Emily saw someone walking down the trail carrying something. The person got closer. It was Marsha, and she was carrying a box. When Marsha got to the clearing, she stopped, and looked around. She did not put the box down. She started walking down the trail, further into the lot.

"Shoot," Emily said.

Emily could not walk through the underbrush fast enough and remain quiet to stay with Marsha. She had to get out to the trail. She left the cover of the bush, went out into the clearing, and moved quickly to the trail. Marsha was gone. Emily ran slowly down the trail, trying to keep the swaying camera from making too much noise. The brush was thick, and she could not see far up the trail, only about 10 feet. She ran around a bend in the trail, and came to another, bigger clearing. Marsha was standing in the clearing, about 20 feet away, facing in the other direction, looking at a turtle who was slowly walking away. Emily took several pictures, but could not get the turtles in the pictures with Marsha.

Emily went a little way back up the trail, and crouched down behind a shrub. The brush was thick. A few minutes later Marsha walked by, heading back up the trail, toward her car. Emily waited a minute and then called Ricardo. "I couldn't get a picture of her holding the turtle. She went to a different clearing."

"Did you get any photos."

"Yea. But none with Marsha releasing the turtles."

"Don't panic. Teddy said she has three turtles. She must be planning on releasing all three. The publicity would be better with three turtles. I bet the turtles are too heavy for Marsha to carry all at once."

"OK. OK. You should see her at her car soon."

Marsha came out of the woods, went to the back of her car and took out another box. Then she went back the woods. Emily was hidden behind a bush at the clearing where Marsha had already released the first turtle. When Marsha arrived at the clearing, she put the box down, and then lifted a gopher turtle out of the box and put it on the ground. Emily got several photo's of Marsha holding the turtle.

As Marsha watched the turtle crawl into the clearing, Emily threw a stick into the woods. Marsha turned her head toward where the stick had landed. Emily came out from behind the bush.

"Did you just see a brown egret fly off?" Emily said to Marsha.

"What? Who the hell are you? Where were you?"

"Sorry to scare you. I was hiding in a bush over there, trying to spot a Yuma clapper rail. You know, the rare birds that someone spotted here a few weeks ago. So did you see anything? I just heard something."

"You scared me. I just heard a noise over there, but didn't see any birds."

"You read about the Yuma clappers didn't you?" Emily said.

"Yes. I like to follow the local nature news."

"So you heard about the turtles too? They were in a clearing about 50 yards back. It was on TV. I think they called them gopher turtles."

"Uh, yea, I heard about them too."

Emily looked into the clearing, and saw two turtles, a gopher turtle and a common Florida snapping turtle. They were a few feet from each other.

Emily pointed at the gopher turtle. "I've never seen one of those around here before. It looks just like the turtles on the TV news. The other one's a snapping turtle. I've seen them before."

Emily walked over to the snapping turtle, and started dangling her fingers about 6 inches from its face, and was giggling, and looking at Marsha.

Marsha watched Emily dangle her fingers in front of the turtle. "Uh. Why are you doing that? I don't think I'd do that if I were you. It might take your fingers off."

"Oh don't worry. I'm as fast as a cat."

Emily looked at the snapping turtle, "You're pretty ugly."

Emily took her eyes off the turtle, and looked up at Marsha. She continued to dangle her fingers in front of the turtle. "Are you hiking?"

"Yes."

"It's a great day for a hike."

"Yes. It is. Why are you taunting that snapping turtle."

"Oh I'm not hurting it. It's fun." The snapper's jaws shot out like a python lunging at a rat. Emily yanked her hand back, and laughed. The turtle recoiled its neck, and Emily put her hand back in front of its beak and dangled her fingers again, this time a little closer than before.

Marsha watched Emily's fingers move. "You do like to live on the edge a little, don't you?"

Emily touched the snapper on its sharp beak, and then quickly yanked her hand back. "Why did you put the gopher turtle here?"

"What? What are you talking about. I didn't."

"It seems like you did."

"The turtle was sitting there when I walked into the clearing."

Emily looked at the box that was sitting on the ground. "That box is brand-new. It hasn't been sitting out here in the rain. If it had, it would be all crumpled up."

"I don't know anything about that box. It was here when I got here."

"No it wasn't."

"It was. Who cares about the box. I'll pick it up and throw it away."

Emily kicked the box away from Marsha and smiled. "I saw you carrying that box down the trail."

Marsha stared at Emily. Then she looked around at the quiet and emptiness of the woods. She looked back at Emily. Emily was nudging the gopher turtle gently with her boot. She was quietly talking to it. "Nice little guy. Why do people do these things to innocent, little animals?" She smiled and slowly shook her head. "Tsk. Tsk. What in the world should we do about this?" She raised her head, looked at Marsha and then gave a big smile.

Marsha moved her eyes to her cell phone, and started to punch in numbers. She stopped before finishing, and said, "I need to go. Good luck with your bird watching."

She started walking quickly across the clearing toward the trail. Emily picked up the gopher turtle, put it in the box and followed Marsha from a distance. Brittany had heard the conversation from her hiding spot, and she walked out onto the trail. She was standing on the trail waiting for Emily as Marsha walked around a bend and saw Brittany for the first time.

Marsha flinched when she saw Brittany. She picked up her pace. She smiled when she skirted past Brittany.

"You're dressed just like that crazy one back there," Marsha said.

"We're in the same club," Brittany said.

"Oh. The nut club?" Marsha shifted to a slow jog.

"Em," Brittany yelled to Emily through the undergrowth. "I'm just up the trail a little bit."

"OK," Emily yelled back.

Emily started jogging up the trail with the turtle bouncing around inside the box. She could not see Brittany or Marsha. The turtle was staring at Emily's fingers holding onto the box, but his head was wobbling.

Emily walked quickly past Brittany, breathing heavily.

"Hey M'am," Emily yelled up the trail. "You forgot your turtles. … Hey, you forgot your turtles."

She stepped out of the woods, onto the grass next to the road. Ricardo was standing behind Marsha's car taking pictures through the back window. Marsha was running toward Ricardo yelling, "Get away from my car! What are you doing? Get away from my car!"

Ricardo ignored her and also took a picture of her license plate. He took a picture of Marsha as she stormed toward him. Marsha grabbed Ricardo's camera, and said, "Give me that. You can't take pictures of the inside of my car. That's invading my privacy!" The two were wrestling with the camera when Emily walked up to them.

"I want those pictures destroyed. That's private — what's in my car is private. Give me the camera."

Emily said, "That's my land. You planted this turtle on my land. Why did you do it? Why did you plant turtles?"

Marsha stopped wrestling for the camera. She looked at Emily, then Ricardo and then watched Brittany come out of the trail. Brittany held up her cell phone and started video taping everyone.

Marsha said, "You're all in this together. You know each other."

Emily said, "We go birding here all the time."

Marsha looked puzzled. "I'm out of here." She opened the car door, got in, and started the engine. Emily stood in front of the car, blocking it. Marsha put the car in reverse. The car started moving backwards. Ricardo and Brittany moved behind it, and banged on the trunk with their hands.

Marsha honked her horn. Emily did not move. Marsha rolled down her window and said, "Get the fuck away from my car, or I'm going to run you over, you psycho."

No one moved. They chanted, "You were planting illegal turtles. You're a criminal."

Marsha sat in the car, staring out her windows. She flung the door open and got out. Emily ran up to her, and Emily stuck her face within inches of Marsha's face, and said, "You're a criminal. You should be locked up. I own that property and you're trying to ruin me."

Marsha said, "I didn't plant any turtles on your property. If you don't get away from my car, I'm going to have you arrested."

"We have pictures of you taking the turtles out of the box and putting them on the ground. On my property."

"BS. No you don't. You couldn't take pictures in that jungle."

"So you admit it."

"Oh shut up. I didn't plant any turtles."

"Yea? Really? So what's that in the back of your car?" Emily was pointing at the gopher turtle in the back of Marsha's car.

Marsha stared. After a moment she said, "That's my pet turtle. There's nothing special about it. It's just a common Florida turtle."

"We'll find out when my biologist friend looks at the picture."

Marsha's mouth was sneering and her forehead was bunched up in large wrinkles. "Let me go, or I'll call the police."

Emily was still holding the box. It was no longer jiggling. The turtle was staring at her fingers. Emily moved her face within a few inches of Marsha's and said, "You bitch. You also planted the gopher turtles that were on TV. You're trying to ruin me. You bitch. You bitch. You bitch."

Marsha punched Emily in the face. Emily dropped the box just as the turtle began to close its beak on her fingers. Emily punched Marsha in the stomach. Marsha smiled and hit Emily again in the face and then the stomach.

Emily was doubled over, and Marsha had turned to get back into her car when a police cruiser pulled up. Officer Jorge Rodriguez got out and said, "What's going on? Are you OK Miss?"

Emily remained bent over, gasping. She had played soccer, and had been good at diving in a close game.

"It hurts officer. She just punched me." Emily pointed at Marsha.

"I want them arrested for harassment and kidnapping," Marsha said. "They wouldn't let me leave. They blocked my car."

"No we didn't," Brittany said. "And look at the garbage she dumped on my friend's property." Brittany pointed to a small pile of Starbucks cups, McDonalds bags, beer cans, cigarette boxes and condoms that Brittany had dumped earlier in the grassy area. "We saw her cleaning out her car."

Marsha looked at the garbage, and lunged at Brittany. Brittany fell backwards, and the officer grabbed Marsha. He handcuffed her. Marsha started yelling, "They framed me. They set me up."

Jorge looked at Emily, Brittany and Ricardo and said, "What were the three of you doing here so early in the day?"

Emily said, "I own the land, and I come by a few days a week to clean up garbage. The town fines me for garbage."

"She's lying. They told me they were bird watchers. This was a set-up."

"Yes, and we were bird watching too," Emily said.

He wrote down Emily's, Brittany's and Ricardo's names and addresses.

"Did you antagonize her?"

"No sir. You know white trash sir — when you accuse them of something, they go after you even if they did it. I saw her dump the trash. She's the first one I've caught. I was lucky. I was hiding in a bush trying to spot those rare birds, the Yuma birds."

Marsha said, "White trash? I can't believe you called me white trash. I went to a great college. My family is rich. I work for an environmentalist organization. I do good. Unlike you. You're white trash, you Florida bitch."

Jorge took Marsha to his cruiser. He had to push her head down to get her in the door as she was screaming insults. Brittany was video-taping it all. Marsha's head disappeared into the cruiser, and Jorge shut the door.

Ricardo said, "Officer, take a look through the back window of her car, and you'll see something interesting."

The policeman looked in the back. "A turtle in a box. A pretty big one. I don't know squat about turtles." He took a few pictures of the turtle with his cell phone. "I'll give the pictures to Fish and Wildlife. Hell, I'll give them the turtles."

"She was planting them on my property," Emily said. "See the turtle in that box over there?" Emily pointed at the box that was about 10 feet away. "We saw her carry the box onto my property, and take the turtle out of the box and put it down on the ground."

"Who saw it."

Brittany said, "Me and her."

Jorge said, "This is a first for me. I don't normally investigate environmental crimes, but I'll pass the evidence along." He took out his phone and made a call. Twenty minutes later a tow truck pulled Marsha's car away.

Jorge said to Emily, "Come over here. We need to talk in private."

They walked away from Brittany and Ricardo.

"Now we're even," Jorge said.

"Why were you so late? I told you yesterday that this bitch might get wild when she was cornered."

"Your friend, the girl, she should have called me sooner. She waited for the woman to get way too worked up."

"Well, whatever. I'm OK."

"So we're even, right?"

"Almost. You need to arrest her. You can't just drop her off at a Winn-Dixie and let her go."

"She'll be arrested. Don't worry."

"You're a Boca cop picking someone up in Delray."

"We talked about that already. I'll say I was in hot pursuit of someone, and so I crossed a few town lines. They got away, and then I ran across some woman who was being attacked by some crazy woman."

"You know what you're doing," Emily said.

"Environmental crap is your problem," Jorge said. "I do assaults. That kind of stuff."

"And prostitution."

"Ha, Ha. Don't worry. I do a lot of work with the prosecutor."

"Prostitution work?" Emily said.

"He's too old for that."

"No man is too old for that. You're all horny all the time."

Jorge looked at Brittany. "Not all the time, but I'm getting horny right now. I love a woman in camouflage. That's why I joined the force."

Emily looked at Brittany, then at Jorge. "You're married, and she's too young for you. By the way, I still have a list of the Johns."

He glared at her. "You had agree to destroy everything to do with that little business venture."

"Only after we were even. We're almost even. The Johns have nothing to do with you and your wife. I had agreed to destroy anything that had to do with you and your wife."

"So help me. If anything turns up that hurts me and my wife, …. Even the list of the Johns. You probably planned to blackmail those guys."

"What a great idea. It hadn't occurred to me. There are a few rich bitches on that list too," she said. "But I wouldn't do that to those poor people."

Jorge laughed. "The prosecutor's a good guy. Marsha is toast. I promise."

"If the press wants to interview you about the arrest, I need you to do the interview."

"Yea, Yea. That sounds easy. But I'll just be following normal police procedures from here on in. And I want the video and the documents that you have been holding. If any copies show up later, I promise, I will make your life hell."

"I'm sure you would. I'll get you the videos and the documents. We can meet somewhere."

"Done?"

"Yes."

Jorge drove away with Marsha and the turtles.

Emily walked over to Brittany and Ricardo. Brittany looked at Emily. "It's nice to finally meet Jorge. He's a looker."

"I doubt if you'll ever see him again," Emily said.

Brittany said, "What now?"

"We're done for today. Just email me the photos and videos," Emily said.

"Emily. This had been the best day of my life. And the car chase the other day was the second best day. How often do you get to do shit like this?"

"Not often enough."

* * *

Marsha was arrested for dumping garbage, assault, transporting a threatened species, and extortion. The prosecutor was sure she would get convictions on the lesser crimes. These were crimes she had settled, or tried and won every day. The evidence against Marsha was easy and solid. The prosecutor was more concerned about the transporting the turtle and extortion charges as they were crimes she did not normally handle. She wanted to be sure she had good evidence. She wanted to win. An acquittal would be embarrassing.

* * *

***

It was difficult for Emily or any outsider to track what was going on in the case. The behind-the-scenes work of the prosecutor was not open to the public. How long would the case take? One month? Nine months? Would Emily have to face bankruptcy first? Marsha's prosecution needed to move fast. Would publicity help push it along?

Emily called her old business professor from college again.

He said, "Please call me Jose. You're a local business person now."

"OK Jose. I was wondering if you might know someone at any of the local newspapers or TV stations."

She told him about Marsha's arrest.

"She planted the turtles too, I'm sure. But the prosecutor is still gathering evidence. I get the feeling that the prosecutor does not have a lot of experience with either environmental crimes or extortion."

"So you want publicity? Why?"

"So the publicity would pressure the prosecutor not to sit on the file."

Jose waited to respond. "I've live here 30 years, and so I know some people at both the newspapers and the TV stations. Not well. But I can call them. Give me the details"

Emily told him what had happened and about the photos and videos that she had.

Jose said, "OK. Let me see what I can do."

* * *

A lawyer friend of Jose's checked on Marsha's current arrest status, and verified that the prosecutor was still looking into the more serious transporting protected species and extortion charges.

Jose called his contacts. Marsha's picture was soon all over the newspapers, TV news and internet. Most of the press loved it. There's nothing like a little scandal to sell newspapers. The non-liberal national outlets news picked up the story as well.

The liberal news sources either hid the story or gave it a different slant. An environmentalist doing wrong!!! Heavens no!! That did not meet the liberal version of how reality was. Only job creating corporations ever did wrong. BSMBC reported that reputable sources had told them the Tea Party had brought the turtles onto the property for assault rifle target practice. They would not disclose their sources. CMM reported that Donald Trump had been seen hiking on the property carrying some unusual boxes. The Washington Posser stated that sources had told them that Sara Palin had been seen on the nearby beach on a jet-ski two days before the turtles were found. They stated she had gained a little weight. They included a photo of a fat woman on the beach with the caption, "Sara Palin's Secret Winter Retreat." On the editorial page there was an opinion article from the paper's editorial staff saying that they had the right, and even the obligation, to lie about conservative politicians because conservative politicians were evil, bad people. There was a vague reference to Hitler and fascists.

* * *

Emily called Carla at Wind Blades, Inc. "When can we close on the sale of the land? I assume you've seen the news. The turtles were planted by some crazy environmentalist. They weren't living on my land."

"I'm comfortable Emily. I'd like to close right away. We want to get the wind blade facility built. Orders are beginning to build up at our other facilities. Here's the problem — our lawyers want to be sure the turtle problem is completely over. They don't trust the State Fish and Wildlife people. We don't want to get a cease and desist order in the middle of construction. Our lawyers have asked Fish and Wildlife for a clearance, and Fish and Wildlife said they can't give it. They are still investigating whether the gopher turtles were naturally living on your land."

"Oh man. This is an endless problem. Of course the turtles weren't naturally living on my land. They aren't natural to South Florida. The were planted."

"Fish and Wildlife wants to see what the prosecutor's is going to do first before they make a decision. It will take time."

"I'll try to find out what's going on at the prosecutor's office. I'll be in touch."

* * *

Emily called her real estate attorney, Rachel. Rachel then spoke to her partner, Samantha Dilochi who specialized in criminal law. Samantha called the prosecutor's office and got the name of Marsha's defense lawyer, Leo Goldstein. Samantha's office scheduled a meeting with Leo.

* * *

Leo's assistant led Samantha into Leo's office. Leo was 58 years old and had been practicing law for 30 years. He had a full head of salt and pepper hair, and a small gut. Samantha was 32 years old and had been practicing law for 4 years. She had blond hair a few inches below her shoulders, was 5 feet 10 inches tall, and 125 pounds.

Leo had made a fair amount of money and had a successful law practice. His office was in a four story office building in downtown Delray Beach. The windows were ten feet long and ten feet high, and gave him an entertaining view of the restaurant and shopping district. On his book shelf were several large, colorful shells, intricate pieces of white and pink coral, sand dollars and sea horses.

"Hi. I'm Samantha Dilochi." She looked at his diplomas hanging on his wall, and then shook his hand.

"Leo Goldstein. Nice to meet you."

She sat down on a chair in front of his desk.

"Please have a seat," he said and sat down behind his desk.

"Nice offices. I like your view."

"Yea, the view is great and so is the location."

"As I told you on the phone, my firm represents Emily Whitney. Your client had a little run-in with Emily."

"I have a lot of assault cases, but this one's a little odd. And not just because it involves two women instead of two guys."

"Yes, it does have some strange circumstances."

"And now it's in the prosecutor's hands, except for my defenses of course. So why are we meeting? Because your client intends to sue my client but will settle the suit for the right amount of money? Or maybe because Earth Zealots has a lot of money and you intend to sue them too?"

"Hmmmmm. That's a good idea. Never thought of that."

"Ha, ha. I'm sure you never did."

"Well, we all like money. But my client does not want to sue. Your client planted some turtles on my client's property, and it's causing problems. Endangered turtles. She wants it cleared up. She has a buyer for the land."

"Marsha has been charged with assault, and dumping garbage."

"And she's also been charged with transporting an endangered species and extortion."

Leo leaned back in his leather chair. "The prosecutor may drop those two. And it's a 'threatened' not an 'endangered' species."

"My information from the prosecutor's office is they'll continue the threatened species and extortion charges. The evidence is strong."

"That's bull-shit."

Samantha glanced out the window behind Leo. "Not BS. Why else did Marsha plant the turtles? She was extorting my client for money. No matter what, she'll have to deal with the extortion charges even if you think you have a defense. Not a lot of fun. Extortion carries some pretty serious jail time. It would ruin her career."

"Marsha never tried to extort money from your client."

"Oh no? Do you think she's told you everything? I have some phone calls recorded that say otherwise. And a text."

"Show me."

Samantha opened a file that was sitting on her lap, glanced at some pages, and then shut it. “I will. But first let’s talk about this from a different viewpoint. Theoretically, if Marsha were to admit that she planted gopher turtles, maybe you could get the extortion charges dropped. Extortion would be really bad for someone like Marsha. Much worse for Marsha than planting gopher turtles. The public likes turtles. Gopher turtles do live in Florida. Unfortunately for your client, they do not live in South Florida. Still they aren’t nasty critters like pythons, and they breed real slowly. They won’t take over like boas did in the Everglades. Look at all the sea turtle protection programs on the Boca beaches.”

“What are you driving at? It doesn’t sound like you’re interested in money.”

“Oh no. We love money. But not by suing your client … at least not right away. At the moment the prosecutor is still investigating the extortion issue. The evidence for the other charges were handed to the prosecutor on a silver plate. The prosecution can’t lose. We have a small window of time here. The prosecutor hasn’t interviewed my client yet. But they are scheduled to meet this afternoon.”

“Your client must be desperate to sell the land.”

“Not desperate at all. The value of the land will probably go up if she holds it. She could wait for Fish and Wildlife to clear her on the turtle issue, which they will. And then she’d sell it at a higher price.”

Leo straightened some files on his desk. ”Emily really wants that land sold as soon as possible. She doesn’t want to wait for Fish and Wildlife. She can’t wait. The bank is breathing down her neck, or they will be soon.”

“No, she’s not under pressure. She just likes to have things go as planned.”

“Yea, that’s what Marsha said. Emily’s a planner. So if my client admits to planting the gopher turtles on Emily’s property, you won’t provide the extortion evidence to the prosecutor?”

Samantha said, “I think the ethics code prevents me from saying it the way you just said it. That came from you.”

Leo stared at Samantha, and then out the window. “I would also need a release from Emily from any lawsuits.”

“I’ll get Emily to give you the release.”

“And get her to drop the assault charges.”

“The prosecutor’s bringing the assault charges, not Emily.”

“Emily could refuse to cooperate as a witness.”

“She’s already given the details on the assault to the cop for his report. She can’t stop cooperating now. Emily needs to stay on the prosecutor’s good side. She hasn’t actually provided any extortion evidence yet.”

“See what you can do.”

Samantha shifted in her chair. “Anyway, the basic deal of Marsha admitting to planting the turtles seems like a no brainer to me. They caught her with a gopher turtle in her car, and there were witnesses who saw Marsha release two other gopher turtles on Emily's property. Marsha's going to get nailed for the turtles no matter what you do for a defense. All we want her to do is admit to something that she's going to get convicted of anyway. She's in no worse position."

"We have our defenses. She's an environmentalist. She was doing turtle reclamation."

"Ha. Ha. With a turtle that is not native to the area? With no permits? On land that was about to be developed? Ha, Leo. I hope she's paid you a big retainer."

"I'll talk to her about your idea."

"I think we both would win, and there really is no down side for anyone. Otherwise both our clients could get screwed. Just in different ways. Emily is scheduled to meet with the prosecutor in two hours. I need an answer from you in an hour."

"I'll call you."

"Sounds good. It was nice to meet you." Samantha got up, shook Leo's hand, and left his office.

Leo stared at her high heels and her butt-cheeks undulate as she walked out. He wriggled his toes. His toe nails were perfectly manicured, and painted a deep red. They were sticking out of his four inch high black leather heals. He stood up and adjusted his silky blue panties that he had bought from the lingerie department at Neiman Marcus.

* * *

Samantha was driving back to her law office when Leo called her.

"Samantha, this is Leo Goldstein. Marsha likes the idea. She'll admit to the turtles."

"Great. Emily will be happy. The deal stands as proposed, right?"

"Yes, as proposed. You need to confirm that you can get the release."

"Don't worry. I'll twist Emily's arm, really hard. I'll call you in half an hour."

"We should do more business."

"I'd love to do more business. "

"By the way, Marsha wants Emily to know that she didn't plant the initial gopher turtles that were on TV. Just the second batch. She would love it if Emily figured out who did the first batch. Marsha's words were, 'then destroy him.'"

* * *

The next day Leo drove to the prosecutor's office to discuss possibly settling the case.

Leo and the prosecutor had been settling cases against each other for years. Leo liked and respected Wanda. Wanda Gomez had been working as a prosecutor for 20 years. She was 48 years old, and had successfully taken a variety of cases to trial, from drunken driving to homicide. She was over-worked but the job was good. She did not have to fish for clients like most lawyers did, and then get them to pay. She earned a high salary and had a good pension and benefits.

Leo and Marsha quickly reached a plea bargain on some of the charges. Marsha would plead guilty to planting both groups of gopher turtles. She also would plead guilty to dumping the garbage. Both deals were contingent on resolving the extortion charge.

"We're part way there, Leo. Let's talk about the extortion. Here's what happened. Marsha wanted money from Emily. She assumed anyone who owned a big piece of land in Delray had money. She knew there was a buyer for the land, and the turtles would muck up the sale. Marsha threatened Emily. Emily refused to pay. Marsha planted the turtles."

"None of that happened."

"Why else would Marsha plant a threatened species on someone's land? If your client pleads guilty to extortion, I'll agree to recommend the minimum penalties to the judge."

"Nice try. What's your evidence?"

"I met with Emily yesterday. She'd be great on the witness stand. Quick, personable, pretty and a local girl made-good."

"Yea? I wonder what Emily really told you. You didn't say that Emily had said that Marsha had demanded money. Did Emily say that to you?"

"That's my business."

"You'll have to tell me eventually under the discovery rules. Wanda, I hope you're not bringing untrue charges against Marsha. You're better than that. We've known each other a long time."

"Of course it was extortion. Why else would someone plant turtles on someone's land? I'll be talking to Emily again. She was holding something back when we first met. I'll get good evidence."

"How about this? There was no extortion. Marsha wanted publicity. Make a name for herself. Get more funding for her non-profit. Rich liberals always throw money at aggressive environmentalists. They feel less guilty for their piles of cash that they inherited from their daddies who had raped the environment."

"Sounds like bull-shit to me Leo."

"Some of those environmentalists are wackos. The rich ones love to give their money away, especially to the politicians. I'm not saying they're all nut-jobs. They've done some fantastic things here in Florida. Helped save the

Everglades. Sea turtle preservation. Other stuff."

"I read that guy Teddy raked in gobs of money for his shop after he was on Fox News."

"You mean the guy who found the turtles a few weeks before Marsha got arrested? He runs Enviro Dogs or something like that?"

"Enviro Bitches I think is the name. More money than you or I will see in a year of work."

"No matter. Your defense is weak. Marsha planted endangered species to get more funding? Try selling that to a jury."

"'Threatened' not 'endangered.'"

"I know. I give money to the Palm Beach County Land Trust every year."

"I give to Earth Zealots every year. Or at least I'm going to start this year."

"Still, Leo, you're really asking me to stretch my imagination with that motive."

"Marsha could get tons of money from new donations. We do have Palm Beach nearby you know."

"You should know. You live there"

"She'd get more money from rich donors than she would get from extortion. Especially trying to get money out of Emily Whitney. Emily's just out of college. I wonder how she got that land to begin with. Maybe you should investigate that. Maybe she's a straw-woman, and someone is laundering money through her."

Wanda said, "Actually, I have looked into how Emily got the land. Sun State bank and Lynn University have a joint program to promote young entrepreneurs. It looks legit."

"Really? I hadn't heard of that? Sounds like a great program. College kids are hurting. My son's having a really hard time, and he went to an Ivy League school."

"Charity money would not go into Marsha's pockets. Charitable gifts would go to her employer. Extortion money would go into her pockets."

Leo said, "Yes, but she'd figure out a way to scoop her hand down into that giant flow of money. Anyway. Back to the extortion charge. I guess Emily didn't give you what you need. You haven't told me of any evidence at all, other than circumstantial."

"She will testify that a guy called on her work phone and demanded $10,000 or he would sabotage the sale of her land. She refused to pay."

"So it was a man. Marsha didn't do it."

Wanda said, "Marsha must have a male partner."

"Marsha did not get caught with that first set of turtles that were on TV. That's when the extortion took place. She got caught with the second set of turtles. She was out for publicity."

"She planted both sets. After the first set of turtles she was surprised that

The Department of Fish and Wildlife didn't immediately conclude that the turtles were living there. So she planted the second set so Fish and Wildlife could make a finding that the turtles had in fact been living on the land."

"Marsha will get a lot more from publicity than $10,000. It wasn't extortion. I could easily sell that to a jury."

"I can't have people running around the county extorting money from people. Especially if it involves a land sale that is going to bring in a well publicized new employer to the area. I don't care that it's only $10,000."

"All you have is circumstantial evidence. Your direct evidence, the phone call, you can't link to Marsha. A jury will believe me. You certainly can't get beyond a reasonable doubt."

Wanda opened her file, and read over Emily's statement. "OK Leo, there are some weaknesses in my cases. If I drop the extortion charge, I want you to agree to the maximum fine for transporting threatened species, and of course for dumping garbage."

Leo looked out the window. "I think we have a deal. I'll get my client to agree. I'll quote her a really high fee for a trial if she rejects the deal. That usually does it."

Both of them made some notes. Leo adjusted his silky panties. His feet hurt in the men's shoes.

Wanda said, "You smell a little like perfume."

Leo sniffed the air. "It must be from my secretary. She pours it on."

"Say 'hi' to your wife for me. We played tennis last Tuesday."

"Yea. She said she had a great time."

"I loved her new outfit. It looked great on her."

"She loves her tennis, but I couldn't figure out why she got home so late."

Wanda smiled and blushed slightly. "We hung out with a friend of hers after tennis for a bit. Lots of fun."

Leo saw her nipples through her blouse getting hard. He got up and walked toward the door. "I'll call you soon."

"See you later Leo."

* * *

Marsha took the deal. The Florida Fish and Wildlife Department reluctantly concluded that someone had put the turtles Emily's land. Marsha's admissions had been clear and unambiguous. 'She had no motive to lie,' the department head had said to his staff.

However, some of the more aggressive bureaucrats in the department had wanted to continue to block the sale. They had hoped and argued that somehow gopher turtles had indeed migrated to South Florida. And that the environment of South Florida would somehow benefit from the turtles. They had wanted to make a name for themselves in the environmentalist community. Their bosses reigned them in, pointing out that the department was not supposed to be anti-business. This was a revelation to them, and it made no sense to them. They set up a secret group to frame their bosses and get the bosses fired. Moderates would not be tolerated. Their liberal professors from college had trained them on how to destroy their opposition. The Saul Alinsky *Rules For Radicals* school of intolerance and viciousness. The professors had used the same tactics in cleansing their university departments of moderate and conservative voices. Our way or the highway.

Wind Blades Inc quickly finished the purchase of the property. The money from the sale paid off the mortgage and costs, and gave Emily a solid profit. Wind Blades Inc immediately cleared the lot, and placed some small prefabricated, temporary buildings on the property. They quickly began producing wind blades in these temporary buildings.

Kelly Carrera and her camera woman from Fox TV stood in front of Wind Blade Inc's temporary buildings. It was late morning and the sky washed a light gray, with the sun trying to break through. She stared into the camera and began broadcasting.

"This is Kelly Carrera from Fox News at the new wind blade facility in the western part of Delray Beach. I'm standing in front of these temporary manufacturing buildings. You may remember my broadcasting here a few weeks ago when gopher turtles were supposedly found on this property. Well it turns out that those turtles were planted on the property by the head of a local environmentalist non-profit. According to the statement that she made to the judge in her court case, her motive for planting the turtles was to get publicity for her non-profit so that contributions would increase. It seems like that has back-fired. Her name is Marsha Goldstein Schwartz, and she is, or was, the head of the local branch of the Earth Zealots environmentalist non-profit. She has pleaded guilty and is currently serving time in jail. It sounds likes there is good money to be made at environmental non-profits.

"To be fair though, we have reported on these non-profits doing wonderful things for our communities, particularly Enviro Hounds from Boca Raton, and their manager Teddy Ceppedy. Teddy was the person who originally had found the gopher turtles that Miss Schwartz had planted on the property. Upon Miss Schwartz's arrest, Teddy issued the following statement: 'It's a shame that some people in the environmentalist field do thing like what Marsha did. It gives all of us a bad name and a black eye. However, I know Marsha quite well, and I can assure you she is a very fine person and has the best interests of the environment and secondly, of our community in mind. She must have been under some unusual pressure to have done what she did.'"

Kelly continued, "The bright side to this story is that this is one of the first light manufacturing plants that has been built in the last 10 years in the Delray Beach area. It is owned by Wind Blades Inc, and it will provide well-paying middle class jobs to about 80 people once it is fully operating. It's an environmentally clean operating facility, and it provides a key component to the wind energy industry. So not only is the Delray Beach area providing some good, well-paying jobs, but it is also helping to fight global warming."

* * *

Teddy and Sam were sitting in Teddy's office discussing a sea turtle egg protection project, when Lucita showed a Florida state trooper into the room.

Lucita stood close to the trooper, and was smiling at him. "Teddy, this gentleman is here to see Sam."

"Hello officer. How can I help you?"

"I have a warrant for Sam Reynold's."

Sam said, "What? I haven't done anything wrong. What's this for?"

The officer handed Sam the some papers, and said "The Florida Fish and Wildlife Department issued the warrant because you transported a threatened species."

"What are you talking about?"

"My job is to serve the warrant, not to answer questions. You need to talk to Fish and Wildlife about the details. The warrant says that you appeared on local TV holding a gopher turtle that you said you had taken off someone's land."

"We have a license authorizing us to move them. Ask Teddy. He's the manager here."

Teddy said, "Yes, officer, I believe we are authorized to move threatened species. We are an environmentalist organization."

Sam said, "Teddy, what do you mean 'I believe?' You said we definitely did."

"We do, I'm sure," Teddy said.

"You need to talk to Fish and Wildlife about that, not me. They concluded that this organization is not authorized to move threatened species. Like I said, I only serve the warrants. The name and number of the issuing party from Fish and Wildlife is on the warrant. Your first step is to call them. You should probably talk to a lawyer first. Your first court date is on the warrant. Good luck gentlemen." He smiled at Lucita, and left Teddy's office.

Lucita followed. "Sir, can I ask you a question?"

Sam said to Teddy, "You 'believe' we are authorized? You dick-head Teddy. I took that turtle because you told me to. I don't want a criminal record. I'll never get a job again."

"I'll check with our central office. I'm certain that they told me we are authorized."

"You mean you never saw the authorization? What if the person you talked to was wrong?"

"Don't worry. Enviro Hounds will stand up for you."

*   *   *

Teddy called his boss who said, "Of course we don't have any blanket authorizations. That's crazy that anyone would think that. It would make no sense. We'd need 52, one for each state, and for Guam and Puerto Rico. Plus each species and each situation would be unique. Imagine all that government red-tape. That's odd that Sam would think that."

"I'll talk to Sam, and find out what he was thinking. I can't have other staff thinking the same thing."

Shoot. The boss will get really pissed if he finds out what I really told Sam.

*   *   *

Later that day Carl from the state Fish and Wildlife Department called Teddy. "We have interviewed Sam in connection with the warrant that we had served on him. Does he report to you?"

"Yes. He does."

"He said that you had told him to pick up and move the gopher turtle. Did you tell him to do that?"

"Ah. I can't remember that well. I was really excited at finding the turtles at that time."

"Try to remember. He's been arrested for moving a threatened species, but if he reasonably had thought he was authorized to move them, that could greatly mitigate the charges, and they might possibly be dropped."

Teddy paused. "Yes, I guess I did tell him that he was authorized to move the turtles. I told him that we had an authorization for all Enviro Hound employees."

"OK. That's consistent with what he told us. You should know that you might be arrested for telling him to move the turtles. We need to review the circumstances. Do you want to retract what you just told me?"

Teddy stared across the room. "No. I did tell him that. Sam's a good guy. He wouldn't break the law."

"Between you and me, and off the record, you probably won't be charged because you work for an environmentalist organization. So don't get too stressed. It's just my job to warn you."

"That's good to hear. You mean if I had done the exact same thing while working for a real estate developer, I'd probably be arrested?"

"Yes. You'd definitely be arrested. Our boss is a big environmentalist. He used to work for some non-profit like yours. He hates developers, and all business people for that matter. Also he never brings charges against anyone who works for a town or state government, even if they break the law. He hates Federal employees though. He always charges them when he can, but they are slippery folks and hard to catch."

"He sounds like King George in merry old England."

"He pretty much is just like King George. Kind of like President Obama letting the wind farm companies slaughter thousands of eagles every year."

"Isn't the law great? Maim and slaughter animals now to theoretically save other animals in the future. From global warming. Or 'climate change' as we call it now. I wonder if other animals will flourish if the earth warms?"

"Who the F knows. You better watch it, you could be hung up to dry for talking like that. Those rich Lefties would cut your funding real fast. And yea, you're right - the law sure is good to us."

Teddy said, "Anyway, how will I know if I'll be arrested or not? I don't want to keep worrying about this."

"If we haven't served you with a warrant in two days, then you're safe — we won't bring charges after that. Unofficially though, you're safe. I'm 99.9 percent sure my boss won't want to charge you."

* * *

Teddy was watching the boats go by on the Intercoastal Waterway from his office, listening to the sounds of sperm whales talk to each other on a DVD his mother had given him for Christmas. It was a crisp April day, and there was a steady breeze blowing up the waterway from the south. He had not felt this relaxed since before his first meeting with Emily. His cell phone rang.

"Hi Teddy. This is Sally."

He hung up. His stomach knotted up.

His phone buzzed. It was a text message from Sally. 'Look at the picture.'

He opened the picture. He saw a frozen bird with its heading sticking out of a plastic bag with several other similar birds next to it.

He texted back, 'So what?'

Immediately his phone buzzed again. A new picture. It showed the same birds, but next to them was a copy of Teddy's college diploma from Brown University.

Then a new text came in. 'That's a Yuma clapper rail, as I'm sure you know.'

Crap. How did she get these?

His phone rang and he answered and said, "We had a deal. Don't break it."

Sally said, "A deal with Emily regarding gopher turtles. This is birds, not turtles. And this has nothing to do with Emily. She doesn't know I've even called you. She doesn't know about the birds at all or the pictures. This is my deal."

"I'm going to drag her into this."

"You'll regret it if you do. I have a very vivid imagination regarding inflicting punishment, especially on misbehaving boys like you."

Teddy clenched a fist. His heart beat faster. He also became aroused. *What's wrong with me?*

"Pictures of dead birds with my diploma. So what?"

"Dead endangered species birds you dick-wad. And you call yourself an environmentalist. 'Endangered,' not like gopher turtles. They were 'threatened.' A much more serious crime."

"They were dead when I bought them. It's not illegal transporting *dead* endangered species." *She's too ignorant to know anything about this.*

"That's funny. I was just reading about an American Indian, I'm sorry, a Native American. I forgot you're an environmentalist. This guy is a medicine man and as part of his ceremony he wore a few bald eagle feathers. The federal gaming people, whatever those nitwits are called, arrested him anyway for possessing bald eagle feathers. He didn't even have the bird's body. Just a few feathers."

"Bald eagles have a special protection. They're above Yuma clapper rails."

"That's BS Teddy. Endangered is endangered."

"No it isn't. Plus, what do you think happens to a Yuma bird when it dies? They don't just leave it there for the coyotes. A biologist takes it back to his lab and dissects it. He doesn't get arrested. He has an authorization. A permit."

Sally paused. "The coyotes eat it before the biologists get it. You seem to know a lot about Yumas for someone who live in Florida."

"The coyotes don't always get them. Not all the time. My agency has a permit to take any dead bird bodies."

"Then you have nothing to worry about when I turn this over to the Feds. I'll email it now. I have their address."

"No, no. What do you want?"

"Just give me $1,000 and we'll be even."

"$500."

"$750."

"That's a deal. You'll destroy all copies. If you don't, I'll have a notarized statement with my lawyer about you blackmailing me. The same deal I have with Emily."

"I know the deal. Yes. The same deal."

"No more blackmail material, right? Nothing else?"

"Nothing else. I promise."

"You're a bitch."

"And proud of it. Don't tell me you don't love it."

Teddy hung up. He was even more aroused now. He left his office to talk to Lucita.

* * *

* * *

The bird watcher that Teddy had almost hit in Nevada had stopped having nightmares about being killed by a white supremacist driving an all-terrain vehicle. The pictures he had taken of Teddy holding the dead birds had come out clearly. The swastika on the ATV was also clear in the picture. So were the birds. Brian, the birder, knew they were Yuma clapper rails and he knew they were endangered.

He was sitting in the living room of his house, relaxing, reading bird articles on the internet. He searched 'Yuma clapper rail' and got various links, including one to a Palm Beach newspaper article. Yuma clappers did not live in Florida. This was a little odd. Brian loved vacationing in Florida, and so was interested in the story. He clicked on the link, and the article on the dead Yuma that had been found on Emily's land came up.

The Yuma clapper was one of his favorite birds. It was so rare, and it lived in his home state. He could not find any more information about the Delray Beach Yuma. The Audubon Society was mentioned in the article. He emailed them.

The Delray Beach Audubon Society emailed back.

'The Yuma clapper rail that was found down here provided a great deal of excitement. Our members tramped around miles of woods and swamps looking for more Yuma's. Unfortunately, they found none. We had a grand old time, though. It was a sizzling topic at our cocktail parties. We are sorry that we are unable to provide you with any more information on this wonderful bird's visit to the Sunshine State. Please stop by if you are ever in the area.'

Brian wrote back, 'Thank you for your response to my inquiry. The Yuma in Delray was truly a very odd find as they are extremely rare even here in their home state of Nevada. It defies the odds. It must have been someone's pet, although I've never heard of anyone having a Yuma clapper rail as a pet. Though admittedly, in Florida I believe there are quite a few unusual pets, and pet owners. I love Florida, and frequently vacation there. Attached is a photo I took of a Yuma clapper rail a few months ago in a marsh on Lake Mead in southern Nevada. I thought you might like the photo.

'Thank you for the invitation to visit. Sincerely, Brian Flashman.'

Brian had enlarged the Yuma clapper rail in his photo.

The Delray Beach Audubon Society wrote back, 'Thank you for the photo of the Yuma clapper rail. It's a beautiful bird. The gentleman in the photo is a prominent environmentalist in Boca Raton, as I'm sure you know.'

Brian read the email. *What would a prominent Boca Raton environmentalist be doing with white supremacists in southern Nevada?*

In a follow up email to the Audubon Society Brian learned Teddy's name and his non-profit. He did an internet search of Teddy, and saw his picture on

Environmental Hound's website. The TV news video of Teddy and the gopher turtles came up. Brian had no doubts that the man who tried to run him over with the ATV was Teddy Ceppedy.

Brian was a respected member of his community. He also had the Nevada Raptor Federation to back him up. So when he went to his local police with his story about being chased by the ATV, the police listened. He showed them his pictures of Teddy and the dead Yumas. The police were particularly concerned about the swastika on Teddy's ATV. They wanted to stop the any white supremacist group early, before it had the chance to grow. The Nevada police issued an arrest warrant for Teddy for attempted murder. They also issued extradition papers to Florida. Teddy soon found himself in a jail in Nevada awaiting trial.

Teddy came from a rich, well-connected New England family. He had personal political connections in Rhode Island who in turn had connections in Nevada. They applied pressure on the prosecutor to reduce the charges. Brian also had connections, and they were strong. He was a local. They also applied pressure.

Teddy eventually reached a plea bargain with the prosecutor for attempted assault. It was a much lesser charge than the original. Teddy faced a one year prison sentence. His defense had been that he had never intended to harm Brian, and that he just been trying to break up the birders' protest against the wind farm. He told the prosecutor that he had never come close to hitting Brian with the ATV.

* * *

The white supremacists housed in the Nevada prison learned that Teddy had impersonated them while chasing bird watchers on an ATV. They accused Teddy of trying to frame them. They did not like the bad publicity of attacking a birder. Some of the supremacists had taken up bird watching as a hobby in prison. It relaxed them. They cut back on their normal drug use. They sympathized with Brian and the Nevada Raptor Federation.

After suffering multiple black eyes, a broken finger, and various contusions and death threats, Teddy settled into a truce with the supremacists. They hated others more than Teddy. In return, Teddy had to cater to some of their needs, and do favors for them. That was less painful than the alternative. His relationship with the white supremacists began to bring back happy memories of his boarding school days in New England. He became accustomed to the prison.

* * *

***

Five months into his incarceration two of his fraternity brothers from college visited him, George and Willy.

George said, "Is it really tough in there Teddy? Is it difficult to get through day-to-day?"

"It was at first. But I made peace with the guys bothering me, and now it's not so bad."

"Glad to hear it," George said. "The Alum have a big croquet match scheduled against the boys in the frat, and we need your wicket skills. It's a month after you get out."

"Oh … uh, yea George. I should be able to make it."

"Super."

Someone ran something hard along the bars in the nearby secured area. The frat boys looked over. A tall, white man with large muscles that were slightly flabby was looking at Teddy.

The man said to Teddy, "We're waiting for you."

"Yea, yea. I know. I won't be long."

The man grinned and walked away.

Willy said, "Who the F is that Teddy? One of your new buddies?"

"Kind of. He's pretty harmless. But you want him on your side."

"Yea, I can see why," George said.

The frat boys looked into the secured area and watched the man talking to two other inmates and a guard.

George turned back to Teddy. "Look, a friend of a friend from the frat is high up in the Nevada prison system, and he'll be able to get you into a minimum security prison. You know, all white-collar criminals. No violent types. A small golf course. A soccer field. They're working on getting a croquet field. Decent food. All you have to do is submit a transfer request form, and you're in."

"I don't know guys," Teddy said. "I'm kind of in a routine here, and there are some guys who protect me."

"Yea, at what cost Teddy?" Willy said. You won't need protection at the other place except from flying golf balls."

"Oh, you get used to it here. It's not that bad."

George and Willy looked at each other, with puzzled on their faces.

Teddy said, "I'd be worried about fitting into a new routine at another prison."

They talked awhile about old times, and future plans. The prison visiting time ended. George said, "You'll think about it, OK Teddy? And we'll keep in touch."

"Bye, bye guys. Thanks for visiting."

Teddy got up and walked toward the door. George and Willy watched him. He was wearing very short, tight, cut-off jean shorts. He walked in short steps and had a little wriggle. He wore flip-flops, and there was a gold ring around his toe next to the big toe.

George and Willy just stared at each other.

* * *

Emily was relaxing on her balcony, smoking a cigarette. It was 7:00 in the evening, cool, and a gentle breeze was pushing the palm fronds back and forth, not far from her face. She dialed her phone. "Hi Mom. It's Emily."

"Hi Honey. It's great to hear from you. How are you?"

"It's going really well. I sold that land."

"That's great Emily! We're really proud of you for hanging in there. I was really worried about you. You and that land."

"Oh Mom. You shouldn't worry so much."

"I know. I know. That's great. I'm so proud of you. Not many people your age are able to flip a piece of property like that. And you did OK?"

"Oh yea Mom. I did great. Easily paid off the bank."

"Well, I hope you made a good profit."

"Yea Mom. It was good."

"Dad will be so happy. He pretended he wasn't never worried, but I know he was. You know, we could have eaten that $50,000 guarantee pretty easily if we had had to. It's a lot of money, but we could have swung it. I hope that didn't bother you."

"It did. But not anymore."

"We'll be flying down in a few months for a week. So we'll see you then. We'll be staying in Miami."

"Can't wait to see you."

"How's the weather been?"

Mom and daughter talked like only a mother and a daughter can talk.

Printed in Great Britain
by Amazon

57927297R00078